TIME GONE AWRY

The scene outside the Scientific Computing Institute on East Fifty-ninth Street had the look of a national emergency. Fire trucks with uncoiled hoses and extended ladders were drawn up in front of the building. Police cruisers were parked haphazardly all over the street, along with a couple of military vehicles from which soldiers were unloading boxes and reels of cable.

Kopeksky stood back and ran an eye over the building. There was something odd about the figures visible inside—something about the way they moved. Their postures and attitudes as they gestured at each other, went in and out of doors, and crossed the vestibule floor, all told of haste and agitation; but there was a strange floating quality to the way they went about it all, as if the whole scene were curiously unreal. And then Kopeksky realized why. The slow-down factor of time in there had grown big enough to see. The people that he was looking at were literally living in a different time. . . .

Books by James P. Hogan

THE CODE OF THE LIFEMAKER
ENDGAME ENIGMA
ENTROVERSE
GENESIS MACHINE
GENTLE GIANTS OF GANYMEDE
GIANTS' STAR
THE INFINITY GAMBIT
INHERIT THE STARS
MINDS, MACHINES, AND EVOLUTION
THE MULTIPLEX MAN
THE MIRROR MAZE
THE PROTEUS OPERATION
THRICE UPON A TIME
TWO FACES OF TOMORROW
VOYAGE FROM YESTERYEAR

OUT OF TIME

James P. Hogan

SPECTRA™

BANTAM BOOKS
NEW YORK • TORONTO • LONDON • SYDNEY • AUCKLAND

OUT OF TIME

A Bantam Spectra Book / December 1993

ISBN 0-553-29971-9

Published simultaneously in the United States and Canada

*Bantam Books are published by Bantam Books, a division of Bantam
Doubleday Dell Publishing Group, Inc. Its trademark, consisting of the
words "Bantam Books" and the portrayal of a rooster, is Registered in
U.S. Patent and Trademark Office and in other countries. Marca Reg-
istrada. Bantam Books, 1540 Broadway, New York, New York 10036.*

PRINTED IN THE UNITED STATES OF AMERICA

RAD   0   9   8   7   6   5   4   3   2   1

To Shuron,
who comes up with crazy ideas like this,
and Morgen,
of course.

00:01

Beep . . . Beep . . . Beep . . .
Beep . . . Beep . . .
"All right,
goddammit."

Beep . . . Beep . . . Beep . . .
The infuriating electronic yelps
continued relentlessly. Joe
Kopeksky groped in the darkness
and stabbed a button at random
among the mess of
incomprehensibility that the
Malaysian instruction leaflet called
the digital calculator/clock/radio/
tape player/coffee maker's
"Control Functionality Console."
A screaming girl with adenoid
problems drowning in a torrent of
hard-rock pounding added to the
din, tearing away the last shreds of
sleep. Kopeksky pressed another
button, any button. Merciful
silence.

Technology's answer to the
hysterical, yappy dog, he reflected
sourly. The chill of mid-November
in New York seeping in from the

streets outside touched his face. There was something unnatural about having to get up on mornings like this—why else would people need to invent gadgets to make them do it?

Beep . . . Beep . . . Beep . . .

"Hi to any listeners out there that we might be getting through to who are wondering if there's any letup in sight to the crazy things that have been happening all over the city for the last few—"

Hiss, squelch, bubble-bubble . . .

Snarling, Kopeksky swung his legs out of the bed and sat up, knocking over the bedside lamp as he fumbled for the switch, and silenced the beeping, babbling digital ensemble with a savage swipe at the thoughtfully provided panic button that turned everything off.

Peace, once again. The apartment greeted him familiarly as he had left it, like a dog that had lain without moving all night: single bedroom; living room with kitchen/dining area; bathroom/shower off the tiny hall inside the front door; den with overfilled shelves of books, files, boxes relating to cases he was working on, and hand-scrawled charts and reminders on the few empty spaces of wall. Kopeksky had a habit of turning information into charts. You could add new information just where it belonged and see how it related to the rest—like having the map of a city instead of having to memorize directions.

All in all, not as much as some had to show after fifty-three years of fighting the terminal disease known as life, he thought to himself, looking around and yawning. But not bad at five-fifty a month in the West Side upper forties; and it was clean and more or less orderly in a lazy kind of way that focused on essentials without worrying too much about making impressions. A lot like Kopeksky's thinking.

Now that he was awake, he regretted having cut off the radio announcer so abruptly. The strange disruptions of time that had been affecting New York City for days were shifting transmission frequencies, causing havoc with radio and TV reception. He checked the time being shown by the digital chronometer on his wrist, with its innumerable other arcane functions that he had given up bothering with. TUESDAY, NOVEMBER 14, the calendar part of the readout said. 7:12 A.M.

Or was it? The display on the now sulkily silent bedside monstrosity said 7:09. He checked the silver-plated windup pocket watch that lay on his bedside table. It was a memento from his father, and his father's father before that, which he had retrieved from a lower drawer in the bedroom chest and taken to carrying with him in the last few days in an attempt to preserve some datum of reference. Its hands were reading, with the solid assurance of the age from which it had come: 7:19. Kopeksky sighed, shook his head, heaved the two hundred pounds that he kept saying he'd have to do something about getting into better shape someday reluctantly to its feet, and headed to the living room.

In normal circumstances he considered himself more or less orderly. But Japlin's report, which he had brought home from the City Bureau of Criminal Investigation to read the night before, was still untouched by the armchair where he had left it, and the phone and utility bills stood unopened in the rack on the table. And when he ate in, he never left the dishes until next morning like this, he reflected as he set up the coffee maker (the old-fashioned, low-tech kind, with one switch and a red light to tell you whether it was on).

This time-glitch business was affecting everything. There used to be time enough to get things done. Now, what in hell was happening to it? Clocks all over the city running at different rates. He'd never heard the like of it. Nothing made any sense.

He tried the TV for an update on the latest situation, but was unable to get any channel. Then he called the Bureau, and, surprisingly, got through on the third attempt. Mike Quinn was on duty in the Day Room that morning.

"Mike, Joe Kopeksky. How's it going?"

"How long do you have, Joe? Hysteria City. It's the usual."

"Got anything for me?"

"Ellis wants you in a meeting at nine sharp, whatever that means. He's got a visitor coming—Dr. Grauss, from out of town. That's all I know."

"What time do you have there, Mike?"

"Clock on the wall here says . . . 7:11."

Kopeksky's digital wrist set was showing 7:19, which meant that the windup back in the bedroom would be at about 7:25. "Well, that gives me almost two hours. Time for another coffee, anyhow."

"Wouldn't be so sure," Quinn replied. "We've just heard from the top floor that whatever else the rest of the city's doing, the Bureau is resetting to Washington EST at eight o'clock. And right now EST's running at 7:25, which says you've got closer to an hour and a half."

Kopeksky sighed. "Okay, I'm on my way."

He hung up and went through to turn on the shower while the coffee was brewing. It was interesting to note that amid the chaos of different time-keeping devices getting out of synchronism all over the city, the one piece that agreed with the broadcast standard from Washington was his grandfather's old windup, with its snap case, Roman dial, and silver chain. That had to say something significant. Just at this moment, though, Kopeksky had no idea what. After drying himself and dressing, he reset the digital chronometer to tally with the windup. Clocks ought to be made of clockwork, he told himself. That's what the word means.

Kopeksky was almost killed on Broadway by a horn-blaring Lincoln charging the line of crossing pedestrians, and again by a cab on Seventh. The sidewalks were practically as dangerous, with running, briefcase-flailing commuters rushing in and out of subway entrances, and every public phone booth seemed to be occupied by a yelling figure gesticulating wildly in the air. No two clocks that Kopeksky saw anywhere said the same thing. Sidewalk vendors were already selling watches hand-carried from Grand Central and set to Grand Central time, which much of midtown had apparently adopted as a standard. Kopeksky found it to be eleven minutes behind his windup, which, if nothing had changed since he talked to Quinn, was in step with the rest of the country's EST. Nope, he told himself as he hurried on, it wasn't going to be one of "those" days, after all. There had never been a day like this one was looking to be.

He reached headquarters by ten minutes before nine and stopped by at the Day Room to check on the latest. NBC had retuned a channel to a frequency that worked, and a group of Bureau people were taking in the news from a portable on Quinn's desk. Kopeksky helped himself to his second morning coffee from the pot on the corner table and moved over to join them. "What gives?" he asked.

"They've just given out a time check as 8:15," Alice, one of the records clerks, replied.

"The airports are closed," Quinn said without looking away from the screen. "Incoming traffic's screwed up trying to synch to the tower times and frequencies. It was still the other side of eight o'clock at JFK, just a few minutes ago." He shook his head. "Oh, man, oh, man. This is wild, wild, wild."

Kopeksky listened to the newscaster. Apparently the retuned channel was being picked up in a few places around the city, but that was by no means true universally. "But I assure you that we're working on it, folks. The latest opinion from our experts here is that it's probably a glitch in the computers somewhere." Kopeksky felt the same kind of reassurance that he did when he listened to TV evangelists or presidential candidates. He took another mouthful of coffee, turned away, and left to make his way up to Ellis's office on the fifteenth floor.

Ellis Wade had arrived steerage through the ranks, not first class or courtesy of any social connections or college degree, which put him at odds with the Bureau's new management style and image. His natural taciturn and laconic disposition did not effectively project the new-age analytical openness that the PR firm hired from Madison Avenue had decided was appropriate to business-school forensics and computer-aided impartiality. Their efforts to enlighten him only deepened the cynicism and suspicion that made him the kind of chief that Kopeksky could live with. The same qualities also made him the only kind of chief that could live with Kopeksky. He was short, but broad and solidly built, with straight, close-cropped steel-gray hair, tanned, heavy-jowled features, and a bear-trap mouth that writhed, pursed, stretched, and compressed itself ceaselessly when he wasn't talking—which was most of the time.

The man sitting next to Wade's desk at once put Kopeksky in mind of his schoolboy imaginings of a Martian: small, but with a disproportionately large and rounded cranium, mildly pink and almost bald, and peering intently through circular lenses that magnified his ocular movements into erratic sweeping motions that suggested an intelligent, wide-eyed octopoid. He was wearing a heavy jacket of plain, light blue tweed and a misshapen maroon tie. Wade introduced him as Dr. Ernst Grauss, from the National Academy of Sciences, Washington, D.C.

"He's been sent to help people here look into this crazy business that's been going on with the clocks," Wade explained. "He deals in . . ." His voice trailed off as he realized that he didn't really know what Grauss dealt in.

"Der physics theoretical it iss, in vich I specialize," Grauss supplied, and by way of elaboration presented Kopeksky with a reprint of a scientific paper that he had authored, entitled *Higher Dimensional Unifications of Quantum Relativity.*

"A scientist," Wade offered, his tone conveying that the title meant as much to him as Kopeksky's expression was registering. Kopeksky sat down in the empty chair in front of the desk and stared back with an okay-let's-hear-it look.

Wade tossed out a hand indifferently to indicate the wall behind him, the rest of the building beyond, and the city outside that in general. "It's all a mess. First they told us it was just something affecting a few TV stations. Then people started getting time checks that didn't add up, so it was the phone company computers too. Now nothing anywhere in the city makes sense. I just came up from Communications. They're having trouble getting through to anybody by radio now. The latest is that JFK, La Guardia, and Newark have shut down operations. All their frequencies are out."

Kopeksky nodded. "I know. I heard on the way up."

The sounds of a door opening and closing came from the corridor outside, then hurrying footsteps accompanied by jabbering voices, fading rapidly. The phone rang on Wade's desk. He answered it irascibly. "Yeah? . . . I said I'd be busy. I'm busy. . . . It is, huh? Okay, fifteen minutes . . . I just said, fifteen minutes." He hung up and looked back at Kopeksky.

"It's as if the time you thought you had suddenly isn't there anymore. Nothing's getting done. Everything's a rush. Nobody's finishing anything."

"Tell me about it," Kopeksky muttered, crushing his empty paper cup.

Wade made a gesture that could have meant anything. "Well, here's something I bet you haven't thought of. Has it occurred to you that the reason why there suddenly doesn't seem to be enough time anymore could be that someone, somewhere, is stealing it?"

Kopeksky stopped in the act of pitching the crumpled cup toward the trash bin and stared speechlessly. "Stealing it?" he repeated. "Someone is stealing time?" Wade nodded heavily, in a way that said it wasn't he who had dreamed this up, and then waved a hand in Grauss's direction. Evidently he himself had said all he was prepared to on the subject.

Grauss wiped his glasses on a pocket handkerchief, then replaced them and brought them to bear on Kopeksky as if making sure that he had his target clearly in his sights before beginning.

"Vor many years now, der scientific vorld hass perplexed itself been by der unpredictabilities unt strangenesses at"—he waved a hand in the air, searching for a word—"untermicroscopic, *ja?*—levels below der atomic—vich are called quantum uncertainty." He barely moved his mouth as he spoke, which with his accent caused his voice to come out as a hiss. "But ve find ven computing eigenfunction connectives across many complex planes, dat der solutions produce conjugate loci vich converge to yield definitions off orthogonal spaces. Unt der quantum reconciliations ve find at ze intersections, unt so obliges us to conclude dat der existence is real. So far is *gutt, ja? . . .*"

Kopeksky just stared, glassy-eyed. "I think what he's trying to say is that the 'other dimensions' that people have been talking about for years really exist," Wade threw in. His tone made it clear that *he* wasn't saying so. He was just saying that whatever bunch Grauss was from were saying so. Wade's accountability ended right there.

"*Ja, ja!*" Grauss nodded several times, excitedly. "Ve haff der universe mitt other dimensions vat ve don't see, but vich can intersect along der complex vectorspaces. Unt vy not, ve ask ourselffs, cannot ziss other universe vich iss here but vat ve can't see, haff its own inhappitants too, who also master der sciences unt der physics, maybe more so zan ve do here?"

"Another guy from NASA called Langlon last night," Wade told Kopeksky. David Langlon was Wade's chief at the Bureau. "They've got a theory down there that we've somehow collided with aliens who exist in another dimension." Kopeksky nodded, having to his surprise extracted more or less that much himself. Wade shrugged. "The way it looks is that time has suddenly started disappearing from the New York area. So one thought is that these guys in the other dimension might be stealing it." Wade showed his palms in a gesture that said it made as much sense as anything else that had been going on lately. The phone rang again. Wade snatched it up, barked "Later" into it, and banged it back down.

Kopeksky jerked his head back at Grauss for some justification. The scientist went on, "Vy, in our vorld, ve spend der lifetimes vorking, vorking, always vorking? Iss to get rich unt make more der money, *ja?* Unt then, vat is it ve vant to do viss all der money? Ve vant it to spend vat little life iss left doing der things ve vanted ven ve vass younger peoples, unt never had der *time*! You see, dat iss vot ve really vant all along, not der moneys at all. Vat ve vant iss der *time*." He spread his hand briefly, as if the rest should have been too obvious to need spelling out.

"But vy spend der lifetime chasing der money around unt around, vich you then haff to use to buy ze time? Iff you possess der capability unt der technology zat iss advanced enough, vy not you simply take der time direct?" Grauss looked from one to the other and concluded, "Unt ziss iss vat, dese aliens, ve conjecturize zey do."

Even after more years than he cared to remember of doing a job that he believed had drained him of all capacity for experiencing surprise, Kopeksky had to strain to keep his composure. Finally he looked back at Wade and protested, "*What* in hell does this have to do with us? We don't know anything about outer space dimensions and quantum . . . whatevers. It's for—"

Wade had expected it and cut him off with a wave. "I know, Joe, I know. But save it. It's not gonna do any good. The situation has been classified a national emergency, which means following up any line that might turn up a solution. It sounds strictly scientific to me too, but somebody somewhere has decided it qualifies as larceny, which also makes it a law-enforcement matter."

Kopeksky shook his head helplessly. "Larceny? . . . Where are we supposed to look for the merchandise? Show me the list of it. I mean, what the hell kind of larceny is this? It's crazy."

"Well, of course it's crazy," Wade agreed. "Why else would the Bureau have gotten mixed up in it? Anyhow, that's your assignment: find out who's stealing the stuff and what can be done about it. Okay? It's straight down the line from Langlon."

Kopeksky sat back heavily in the chair. "That's it? You're sure you don't want anything else? I mean, do you need it before lunch, or would afterward be okay?"

"For now, go and do some head-scratching and see what kind of a strategy you can come up with. We'll get together and go over it this afternoon," Wade answered, unperturbed.

"But what kind of help can I expect to get on it?" Kopeksky demanded. "What kind of resources? Who are the contacts? Don't I even get some idea of that to take back to the office?"

Wade was looking at his watch. "Gee, is that the time already? Oh, yeah, that's right. They reset to EST. I've got another appointment waiting already."

Grauss rose to his feet, revealing a miniature frame that nevertheless seemed to be all limbs, giving Kopeksky the feeling that it might be about to come apart at the joints. "I must der train to Hartvord catch, unt den from zere fly der plane back to Vashinkton," he announced. "A pleasure to be meetink you it hass peen, Mr. Kopinsky."

Wade spread his hands apologetically. "Sorry, Joe. It looks like there isn't time."

Deena Rosenberry, Kopeksky's junior partner, rummaged about in the confusion of billfold, checkbook, notes, envelopes, clippings, pens, and makeup paraphernalia filling the bulging purse that she always placed at arm's length on the floor by her desk, and which Kopeksky was certain contained everything she owned.

She was a good six inches taller than he, lean-bodied and long-limbed, and uncoordinated to the verge of creating a new art form. And yet she was graced with potentially fine looks—if she'd only learn how to go the right way about helping them a little and pick the right clothes. The pointed chin, high cheekbones, and straight, narrow nose that was a shade too long made her face heart-shaped in front and interestingly angular from the side; but her hair, full-bodied and dark, was somehow always too stern when she tied it up, and fell all over the place in riotous disarray when she wore it loose. Today, she had on a dark green skirt that was too old for her mid-thirties, with a mauve top that was too young, and a jacket that went with neither. The brown leather walking shoes were good quality, practical for her kind of work, eminently sensible for New York in winter—and should have been banned as an offense against public decency for any woman under forty-five.

Eventually she retrieved two laundry tickets from one of the purse's innumerable pockets and pouches, and transferred them to a pocket in her jacket. "A couple of sweaters that I meant to pick up on the way in, but I ran out of time," she explained. To anybody who wasn't used to her, it would have sounded as if she hadn't heard a word that Kopeksky had been saying. But then she went on with barely a pause to hint of any changes of continuation, "It is November fourteenth, right?"

"It was the last I heard . . . unless things have gotten really fouled up out there," Kopeksky replied from the other side of the office that they shared three floors down from Wade's. He was sprawled back in his chair with his feet on the desk and hands propping his chin, contemplating his shoes. That was the other thing: her mind seemed to share her body's proclivity for doing several disconnected things at once—and somehow disentangling them all successfully in the end, no matter how disconcerting it was to anyone watching.

"I mean, it isn't April first or something," Deena said, pushing the purse back to its place. "This isn't somebody's idea of a crazy joke?"

"Oh, it's crazy all right. But that strudel wasn't joking. And maybe it's true. . . . What else has anyone got to explain what's going on out there, all over the city?"

Deena moved piles of files and typescripts to

clear some space amid the layers of documents that covered her desk like geological strata. Somehow, a page of notes on the story that Kopeksky had related, heavily underscored in places and adorned with query marks and aside thoughts captured in circles, had materialized in the midst of it all while the search for the laundry tickets was in progress.

"What did he mean by a technology that's advanced enough?" Deena asked, checking over what she had written. "Is he talking about these aliens having some kind of machine that sucks time out of our universe like . . . like a vacuum cleaner, and then spews it out in theirs—like a siphon or something?"

"You tell me."

"But if that's so, then what is anyone supposed to do? The way I remember it, the whole thing about other dimensions is that they're at right angles to everything you can think of, which means you can't even imagine them, let alone affect what happens in them."

"Well, they seem able to affect what happens with us," Kopeksky pointed out, "so why not the other way around?" He moved his feet off the desk, stretched himself back, and clasped his hands behind his head to stare up at the ceiling. "As if we didn't have it bad enough here already. People getting hernias and heart attacks chasing to airports to catch planes, and worrying about filing taxes on time. . . . I mean, who are these aliens? Do they live in fancy villas or something, get to watch a movie and finish the books they put down, play golf, take in a ball game, stop by at their friends', and still have plenty of time to go fishing with the grandchildren? Is that what they're at? . . . And doing it all on *our* time—time that they've stolen from us? Well, hell, I don't like it. There has to be something that someone can do."

"Like what?" Deena invited, and then went on without missing a beat, "Oh, yes. I've been trying a number all morning, and it's busy—I mean not just right now, but all the time. Can you tell me if there's some kind of fault?" She was holding a memo pad and had picked up the phone.

"Well, let's take things right back to the beginning," Kopeksky said. "What do you do when you suspect that something is being stolen? You mark it somehow, okay? Or watch it, or maybe you set up a stakeout. . . ." He pulled a face. "Nah. Nothing like that's gonna work. How do you start?"

"Oh, really? . . . Them too, eh. So what do you have right now?" Deena scribbled something on a slip of paper. "Okay." She put down the phone and looked over at Kopeksky. "See, all those things depend on some kind of information getting back to you about the actions of whoever you're out to nail. But with what Grauss is talking about, there isn't any way that it can. What we've got is a communications problem." She indicated the piece of paper that she had written on and changed the subject like a stage impersonator switching hats. "It isn't just the phone company's time checks, either. The clock at the exchange I just talked to is at 10:14 right now. Calls have been coming through in what to them is less time than we're seeing, and that's why they're jammed."

Kopeksky looked at his old windup. It read 10:53. The digital watch that he had set to EST time at 7:25 when he talked to Quinn immediately after getting up was now three minutes behind at 10:50. Out of curiosity he called down to the Day Room to inquire if they still had the channel from NBC. They did. What time was NBC giving? 10:22. So the telephone exchange was eight minutes behind NBC, which was thirty-one minutes behind EST (assuming Kopeksky's windup was still reading EST), but the digital watch had dropped three minutes behind the windup since he synchronized them both early that morning. He noted the figures down but didn't even try thinking about what they could mean.

"Well, if Ellis says it's an emergency and to try all approaches, why don't we try what the scientists down in Washington won't be trying?" Deena suggested. "If we're talking about contacting places that you can't normally contact, let's talk to some psychics."

"Psychics," Kopeksky repeated, looking at her. His tone asked why not the Tooth Fairy and the Easter Bunny too, while they were at it?

"I know it's a weird idea," Deena said, "but the whole thing is weird already. Besides, if there really is something to these aliens that Grauss is talking about, then maybe there's something to psychics too." She shrugged. "Anyhow, we won't find out any other way. And it is somewhere to start. Got any better ideas?"

Kopeksky thought about it. "It might give us a new angle on what time is, if nothing else," he conceded finally. "Aren't they supposed to have oddball notions about things like that, as well as catching ghosts and talking to dead grandmothers?" He warmed more to the idea as he thought it over. "You could be right. Maybe that's what we need—some new angles on what time really is. What other kinds of people know anything about it? . . . Philosophers are into stuff like that, aren't they? Better put them down if we're talking about making a list of experts."

"Mathematicians," Deena said. "There must be dozens of them in the colleges and universities around the city."

"Astronomers," Kopeksky said. "That's an obvious one."

"Maybe a religious expert or two?" Deena suggested. "If we're looking for unusual angles . . ."

Kopeksky gave a what-the-hell shrug and nodded. "Why not one of them Eastern Yogi Bears? You know, the guys who stand on their heads and think about navels. Aren't they supposed to fly around in astral dimensions or something?" At that moment his phone rang. It was Ruth, Wade's secretary, letting him know that Wade had rushed off on something urgent and wouldn't be able to see him that afternoon.

"Looks like we've got the afternoon clear," Kopeksky told Deena as he replaced the receiver. "Okay, we'll spend the rest of today going through contact lists and making calls, and tomorrow we can start interviewing. First we need to start with some research. That's your department. Okay, let's get to it. There's work to do."

Deena surveyed the devastation of her workplace. "Joe, where does all this mess come from?" She sighed. "Eskimos may have a hundred different words for it, but I'm snowed. Where does the time go?"

Kopeksky shrugged and picked at a tooth with a thumbnail. "File a lost property report," he suggested.

00:03

By next morning, the various official measures that had been introduced to bring some order to the situation had shown mixed results, since nobody could agree whose official measures to go by. Government departments had been instructed to follow EST time as broadcast from Washington. But that was of little benefit, since after setting to the EST standard, offices in different places would then fall behind it at different rates, which in any case turned out not to be constant. Typically the lag was fourteen minutes per (EST) hour at the Defense Department on Varick Street, twelve minutes at NASA on Broadway, eight minutes at City Hall, and seven minutes at the Justice Department. Meanwhile, NBC was sticking to a twice daily update schedule of its own that meant losing three hours out of every twelve, but Grand Central

Station had fallen into line with the power companies, who were having to run their generators faster to compensate for delivered frequencies falling by up to twenty percent. At JFK, the situation had improved overnight after the shutdown and reversion to caretaker operations only. Whereas the previous morning's chaos there had been caused by a time discrepancy of over thirty percent—one of the greatest measured anywhere—now it was less than ten.

At 11:45 sharp by his pocket windup, Joe Kopeksky arrived for his final appointment that morning at a converted Upper West Side block of pricey apartments on a corner overlooking the Park, which contained the town residence of Inigo "The Extraordinary" Zama. Psychic, clairvoyant, medium, telepath, foreteller of the future, gazer across distance, and seer into realms unknown; the man for whom, the flap copy on the latest collection of his feats and revelations to hit the best-seller lists proclaimed, "the Universe holds no secrets."

"Where did you say you were from, Mr. Kopalsky?" he inquired as the woman who had answered the door showed his visitor in. It was a large, bay-fronted room with heavy drapes and leafy-embroidered furniture finished with tassels and raised cord welts. A white marble fireplace set between Ionic columns and surmounted by a huge, gilt-framed mirror divided the wall opposite the window. An oval mahogany table standing below a chandelier dominated the center of the room, and a marble-topped stand in the window bay supported a fish tank. On all sides were shelves and cabinets carrying a varied collection of books, antique European ornaments, and curios.

"It's Kopeksky," Kopeksky said. "City Bureau of

Criminal Investigation. We talked on the phone yesterday. Today is Wednesday."

Zama had a balding head fringed by hair that was turning white and a matching mustache that he curled at the ends and waxed, making him look like the Monopoly man. His eyes had an unnatural glint to them, due either to the unearthly powers that dwelt within or to reflectively tinted contacts. He was wearing a silk robe carrying an elaborate oriental design of pointy leaves, birds, and dragons. He dismissed the secretary, whom he addressed as Sonia, and moved around the center table toward the open area before the fireplace, stopping on the way to gaze at the fish tank by the window. The fish swimming around within it looked to Kopeksky like gray cigars with rounded tails resembling duck's feet at one end, gloomy faces trailing overgrown warts at the other.

"A species of catfish that inhabits muddy waters where the visibility is practically nonexistent," Zama commented. "Nevertheless, it manages to 'see' quite well by sensing changes that obstacles and other creatures produce in the electric field surrounding it. A perfectly natural phenomenon, but beyond the comprehension of other fish not equipped to share its abilities. An interesting analogy to the powers that lie beyond our own everyday human senses, wouldn't you agree?"

"Can they talk to pigeons?" Kopeksky asked.

Zama blinked. "I beg your pardon?"

"I'm interested in communicating with places that are out of this world. People tell me that's what you do."

"It is one of numerous fields that appear separate on this plane but which stem from the same nexus of association manifolds in the higher ether," Zama said.

"The kind of assistance that I normally offer to police departments is in locating missing persons or objects. The precedent is well established, you know."

"We're not exactly talking about persons or objects," Kopeksky started to explain; but as if not hearing, Zama steered him to the large table in the center of the room and picked up a silver chain of finely formed links, attached to a multifaceted crystal sphere. The sphere was elongated on one side and tapered to a point, like a pendulum bob.

"This is a technique that extends back through adepts over many centuries," Zama said. "Science has never been able to explain it."

"That's great, and I'm sure there are guys in other departments who—"

"Do you have a dime and a penny?"

"A what?"

"Some loose change. I haven't dressed yet, and I'm not carrying any in my robe."

"Probably. Let me see. . . ." Kopeksky felt in his right-hand pants pocket and produced an assortment of coins. Zama selected a dime and a one-cent piece and placed them on the table about eight inches apart.

"Every object possesses a characteristic aura, which is an induced disturbance of the permeative-vibrational field that flows everywhere from the galactic poles," he explained, suspending the chain above the dime. "An individual who is sensitive to the fluctuations unconsciously translates the received impressions into muscular actions, which the pendulum amplifies and makes visible." As Kopeksky watched, the crystal bob swung to and fro in a pattern that quickly became circular. "Note, clockwise: the signature of nickel and other silver metals," Zama said. Then he moved the pendulum over to the cent. "But

cupric and ferrous alloys produce a linear response."
The bob obliged by swinging backward and forward.
"It is also effective in discriminating most other minerals, as well as colors, drugs, plants . . ."

"How about places?" Kopeksky said again.

"Ah, you mean spirit communications," Zama said, nodding. "You are in need of information from the deceased. Yes, I have some experience of that."

Kopeksky shook his head. "Dead guys don't have anything to tell me. I'm talking about aliens in other dimensions."

Zama frowned for a moment and turned away from the table. "Please understand that my work demands a broader terminology than that which suffices for the more restricted, orthodox sciences," he said. "There are many structures of existential continuum containing energy-information equivalents capable of being orthorotated into our own reality sphere. The parametric probes necessary to establish an identification may take time, and my time is in high demand and expensive." He glanced back at Kopeksky in the gilt-framed mirror above the fireplace. "I, er, take it that you are here officially . . . on Bureau business?" In other words were they talking a taxpayer-funded checkbook?

Kopeksky decided that he wasn't going to learn much about communicating with aliens. "Forget about it. Let's talk about time," he suggested instead. "Isn't that something you're into? What can you tell me about that?"

"Time, Mr. Kopeksky?" Zama swung around and voiced the word imperiously, as if there were more contained in the term than they could cover if they had all week.

"What clocks tell ... The stuff there's never enough of when you've got a plane to catch."

Zama made a sweeping gesture toward the window. "The fabric of it is rending apart as we speak. You know what's going on out there. It's the nuclear power plants that are doing it—so-called scientists meddling with forces they don't understand."

Kopeksky nodded sharply. "Exactly: what's going on out there. That's what I'm interested in! We know that somehow time is messing up. But what *is* time?"

Zama turned his palms upward contemptuously. "To me it doesn't exist. It is a fabrication. A necessary construct of lesser developed psyches that are not yet capable of comprehending the totality. So they must apprehend piece by piece, in infinitesimal slices. But for me the future lies as a map to be read. Would you like to see a demonstration of elementary precognition, Mr. ... Kopeksky?" Zama picked up a wooden box from a shelf and opened its lid to reveal a pair of dice.

"Isn't that the kind of thing that magicians do at kids' parties?" Kopeksky queried.

Zama snapped the box shut and tossed it back down on the shelf. "I'm sorry, I thought that you had come here to discuss something serious," he said in a pained voice. "Those are mere entertainers."

"I know *they* are," Kopeksky agreed. "But if you've got the real thing, I'd have thought there'd be more point in using it for something that matters. For instance, who can you tell me about, somewhere in those offices out there right now, maybe, that shouldn't try driving home tonight? Or who oughta call in a contractor about the roof instead of going up a ladder and trying to fix it themselves? Know the kinda thing I mean?"

"Regrettable, but inevitable." Zama showed his

hands and sighed. "Grief has always been with us. It sounds callous, I know, but really, what would be the true worth of averting one individual's tragedy in this complex web we call life, that involves billions? I could devote twenty-four hours a day of the rest of my life to such noble causes, and it wouldn't add up to making a scrap of difference that would matter. No, Mr. Kopeksky, I must conserve my energies for more important works."

"You mean like finding dimes with pendulums?"

"That was just a trivial illustration," Zama said, sounding irritable. He moved forward, away from the fireplace. "But the same technique can find deposits of valuable ores, oil fields . . . You see, benefits that will affect millions of people. Not many people know how much money the major companies are investing in this kind of thing nowadays."

That was probably true, Kopeksky reflected. He sure as hell didn't know. It could have been nothing, and Zama wouldn't have lied. "You mean it still works, right down through all that rock?" He sounded impressed.

"Oh, absolutely," Zama assured him loftily, moving forward again and sounding on firmer ground. "Space, matter, and distance are no objects."

Kopeksky gestured down at the top of the mahogany table, where he had covered the two coins with a handkerchief from his other pocket. "Then obviously this wouldn't be any problem. I'm sure you're right, but you know how unimaginative policemen are. Just to satisfy my personal curiosity, can you still tell which one of these is the dime?"

Zama stopped and looked down uncertainly. "You expect me to waste my time on parlor tricks?" He was trapped, and his voice betrayed it.

"It would be too bad if I had to go back and report a failure, wouldn't it?" Kopeksky answered with a shrug. "Especially with all those lost people and objects they've got on the files back there."

Zama extended his arm to hold the pendulum over one end of the handkerchief. He hesitated, then moved the pendulum to the other end. Kopeksky's mouth twitched, and after a second or two the bob began tracing a circle.

"That's it?" Kopeksky inquired, cocking an eyebrow. Zama nodded stiffly. Kopeksky turned back the end of the handkerchief. Sure enough, the coin lying there was a dime. He nodded approvingly. "Not bad."

Zama moved the pendulum back to the other end, where it promptly changed its motion to a straight line. "And there is the penny," he pronounced, his former self-assurance now restored. "As I said earlier, just a trivial illustration. But it proves the principle, you see."

"You mean about the permeative-vibrational field that flows from the galactic poles? That was what you called it, right?"

Zama's eyebrows raised a fraction in surprise. He nodded. "Precisely."

Kopeksky lifted the remainder of the handkerchief to reveal a second dime. He shook his head sadly and clicked his tongue. "Oh, dear. Well, I guess nothing in life is perfect, eh? Maybe you just need to work on it a little more before you file for the patent."

Zama glared down at the evidence, his waxed mustaches bristling. "Interference," he pronounced. "The B line subway goes right under here. The metal of the rails interferes with the reading."

"Yeah," Kopeksky said, gathering up his things and heading for the door. "They dig 'em real fast these days."

00:04

"They were all yo-yos," Kopeksky told Deena across the booth when they met in a deli on Lexington to compare notes forty (windup) minutes later. "I learned about birthday-party tricks and electric fish. Might as well have stayed home and read fortune cookies. How'd it go with the philosophers?"

Deena shuffled among the notebooks and papers littering the tabletop between her coffee mug and plate with its half-eaten pastrami on rye. The purse that accompanied her everywhere was on the seat next to her, and a nylon carry-bag, bulging with reference books, had appeared alongside it.

"I talked to Morton Bridley at Columbia, Schumann at Fordham, Arnold Cuppenheim at NYU . . ." She turned a page, scanned over the scrawl on the one beneath, then delved among some loose papers covering the sugar bowl. "And a

guy called Chaim Mendelwitz from the Jewish Theo-
logical Seminary that one of them recommended.
Gellsard from Rockefeller had to rush off in a panic
about something, but I did get to see another guy there
called ... Hunter, was it? ... Oh, yes, here we are:
Herman Hunter."

"So what have we got?" Kopeksky grunted. On
days like this it was easy to feel inadequate.

Deena took another bite from her sandwich and
then searched around again, finally retrieving a wad of
handwritten sheets from beneath her coffee mug. "One
of the earliest mentions of time as a discrete concept is
in Aristotle's *The Categories*. He listed it as one of
them."

" 'Them' what? Categories?"

"Yes."

"He was some Greek, right?"

"Fourth century B.C."

"Okay, so what's a category?"

"Nobody seems to know. Kant and Hegel use the
term too, but they're all different. Russell described
them as being 'in no way useful to philosophy as rep-
resenting any clear idea,' so maybe it doesn't matter.
But in his *Physics*, Aristotle says it's 'motion that ad-
mits of numeration.' That means motion that can be
counted in numbers."

"Why? What's so special about numbers?"
Kopeksky asked.

"It isn't clear," Deena answered. "It seems like
Aristotle just had this thing about numbers. He wondered if time could exist without there being souls
around, since he figured there couldn't be anything to
count unless there was somebody to count it. And that
proves time couldn't have been created."

Kopeksky stared at her fixedly while he poked at his teeth with a pick. "Uh-huh."

Deena picked up the next sheet. "But Plato didn't agree. According to him, the creator wanted to make an image of the eternal gods. But that wasn't possible—for it to be eternal, I mean, I guess because that's what gods are—so it had to move."

"What did?"

"The universe. That's what the creator was creating."

"Oh. Okay."

"And that's where time came from. Without days and nights we wouldn't have thought of numbers. In other words God made the sun so that animals could learn arithmetic . . ." Deena caught the expression on Kopeksky's face and hastily switched to another section of her notes.

"St. Augustine also thought that time came out of nothing. See, he worried about why the world wasn't created sooner. And the answer he came up with was that there couldn't have been any 'sooner.' So time had to have been created at the same time everything else was."

"Brilliant."

"But there were some parts of his system that he had problems with."

"Really?"

"Yes. First, he figured that only the present really *is*. But he had no doubt that the past and the future really exist too. So here was an apparent contradiction."

"Did he come up with a brilliant answer for this one too?"

"Of course. He was a saint."

"What was it, then?"

"The past still exists as what you remember, and

the future exists already as what you expect to happen. So really there are only a present of things past, a present of things present, and a present of things future. And that explains it: they only exist now, and they're all real."

Kopeksky's face registered a conviction that fell somewhere short of total. "What if what I expect doesn't get to happen?" he asked. "Is it still real?"

"Er . . . it doesn't say."

"Scratch one saint. Who's next?"

"Spinoza didn't think time was real at all, and so any emotions that have to do with the future or the past are contrary to reason. Only ignorance makes us think we can change the future."

"If we buy that, we might as well turn in our badges. What else?"

Deena separated some insurance papers from among her notes and stuffed them into the top of the purse beside her. "Schopenhauer claimed that the world is all an objectification of will. The aim of existence is total surrender of the will, in which all phenomena that are manifestations of it will be abolished. That includes time and space, which constitute the universal form of this manifestation. Thus there will be no will: no idea, no world. The only certainty is nothingness."

Kopeksky bit the end off a pickle and considered the proposition. "What does that mean?"

"I don't know. . . . Hegel didn't believe in space and time either, because they involve separateness and multiplicity, and only the whole can be real. . . . Hume defined it as one of seven kinds of philosophical relations, but then he got kind of tangled up over whether we see the causes of things, or only the results of causes. . . . Kant thought it was real but subjective: it exists in your head, not in the world you're looking at."

"How'd he figure that?"

"It kind of came out of a general theory he had about perceptions being due to two parts: the part of what you think you see that's really out there, and the part that you add to it inside. Like, if you wear red glasses, you see a red world. But the red that you see is something you carry around with you. The space and the time that we think is part of the universe are really orderings that we impose on it because of the way our minds work."

Kopeksky thought about it. "So how come we've all got the same color lenses?" he challenged. "Why does everybody see the roof on top of the house instead of the other way round?"

Deena nodded as she searched under the papers for her pen. "A lot of other philosophers asked the same thing."

"So what did he tell them?"

"He didn't have to. They only got around to asking about it after he was dead."

Kopeksky sat back in his seat and stirred his coffee for a while. Deena began tidying her notes back into some semblance of order. "Out of curiosity, what did all these guys manage to agree about?" he ventured finally.

"Not much."

Kopeksky nodded in a way that said it was what he had expected. "Well, I guess we had to try."

"So where do we go now?" Deena asked.

He raised his cup and drank moodily. "Back to basics and start at the scene of the crime. Or in this case, scenes. Some of the biggest time lags we've heard about were at the airports, before they closed, the TV networks, the phone company, and the utilities. We talk to them and see what we can dig up there."

"That's what I figured." Deena rummaged in her purse again and found a notebook. "I've already got us some leads in those places."

"Fine. Then I'll finish working the list we've already got," Kopeksky said. He shrugged and produced the check, which he had kept out of harm's way in his breast pocket. "Might as well see it through now." His tone said that he didn't expect to get much out of it.

"Who've you got next?" Deena asked.

"The priest." Kopeksky's mouth moved expressionlessly. "Why not? What the hell, it can't get any nuttier."

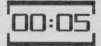

00:05

Kopeksky found the church of St. Vitus in the Fields hidden between a pile of sooty-windowed offices and the rear of a warehouse in the jumble of streets that dated from the beginnings of New York City, before planners discovered right angles, on the Lower East Side below the Manhattan Bridge. Its unassuming frontage of weathered stone stood sandwiched between soaring perpendicularities of concrete and glass, looking as if year by year it yielded a little more to the encroaching city, and one day would be squeezed out of existence entirely.

A housekeeper with gray hair and a robust smile answered the door to the presbytery, which was situated behind the church along a narrow passage fenced from the street by iron railings. She took Kopeksky's coat and hat, stated that it was "a grand day for

November, especially at this time of year," and showed him upstairs to the study of Father Bernard Moynihan.

It was a warm and cozy room, with oak-paneled walls and a deep maroon carpet. Solidly made bookshelves extended to the ceiling on either side of a leather-topped desk angled across one corner by the window, and two armchairs faced a cheerfully blazing fire. Moynihan himself, in shirtsleeves, was standing before the hearth, warming his back, when Kopeksky entered. Kopeksky put him at fiftyish. He was a good five-ten in height and hefty, with florid, craggy features and iron-gray hair combed straight back. As the housekeeper moved around to add more smokeless briquettes to the fire, he came forward a pace and brought his hands around to rub them together.

"Mr. Kopeksky, who has the job of picking up the pieces when we fail at ours." He motioned with his head to indicate the clock on the mantelpiece behind him. "And right on time. That seems to be quite an achievement these days, from what we've been hearing." The brogue was soft and diluted by years of living this side of the water—but definitely present.

Kopeksky pulled out the pocket windup and compared it. They matched to the minute. "I'll be darned," he said. "It's the first time that's happened."

"Ah, is that a fact, now?" Moynihan answered. "Then this must be the first time you've been near a place with any sanity in it for days." A hint of humor around the mouth, Kopeksky saw, and more about the eyes. Not a flake, he decided. Flakes took themselves too seriously to be able to afford any concession to humor.

"Is that what it's all about, then?" he replied. "Sanity?"

"Ah, sure ye've only to look at the places it's happening in and ask yourself what it is they've got in common. But first things first. Will you take a cup of tea, Mr. Kopeksky?"

"Any chance of coffee?"

"Certainly, if you prefer. But I'm not talking about the tea bag floating in bathwater that they try fobbing you off with over here. It's the real stuff I'm meaning, made boiling in a pot the way God meant it to be. One of the only two good things that ever came out of England." The priest's eyes were clear and alert, and gave the impression of already having absorbed all there was of Kopeksky to be divined outwardly.

"Okay, I'll try it," Kopeksky conceded.

"A pot of tea for two if you would, please, Ann," Moynihan said as the housekeeper moved toward the door.

"And biscuits, is it?" she inquired.

"Cookies," Moynihan translated.

Kopeksky shook his head. "Not for me." Ann went out, closing the door behind her.

"Please." Moynihan waved Kopeksky to one of the armchairs and settled himself down in the other. The fire felt warm and relaxing after the drab dampness of the day outside.

"Some fields," Kopeksky said, referring obscurely to the fact that the church could have been called something more appropriate to Lower Manhattan. It was a test to see if he was dealing with somebody who caught on quickly.

"Oh, I think it was a name that somebody brought with them from the old country a long time ago now," Moynihan told him. "There might have been some truth in it then too."

Kopeksky grunted. "So what was the other good thing that came out of England?"

"Oh, this stodgy thing of theirs that they call reasonableness and common sense. Not a bad idea, I suppose. They tried to import it, you know, but it didn't grow. In Ireland it's an exotic—not suited to the climate or the soil."

"You sound like you know something about plants," Kopeksky commented.

"A little," Moynihan agreed. "In the years of my wilder youth I spent some time in missionary work, mainly in Africa, which of course entailed dabbling in all kinds of biology. But my main interest was in entomology rather than botany."

"That's bugs, right?"

Moynihan nodded. "I started out as a medical man—insect-borne diseases. But then one day I got to thinking, what's the use of saving lives if it isn't so that people can learn to live them better? And that was the side of things that seemed to be in need of the most help." Kopeksky nodded that he both understood and agreed. Moynihan glanced across. "Insects are still what you might call a hobby of mine, though. In fact, I keep a colony of termites in the basement here. Fascinating, the habits of the social insects . . . Would you like me to show them to you?"

Kopeksky held up a hand apologetically. "It sounds great, Father, but I gotta take a rain check. Maybe another time."

"Of course. You're doubtless caught up in all that bedlam that's going on out there. Then tell me how I can help."

Kopeksky had by now come to the conclusion that he wasn't going to find any sudden illumination as to the true nature of time, and that even if he did, it wouldn't get him anywhere. However, he still hadn't given up on the notion that the way to reach Grauss's aliens might be through some unsuspected means that could have been staring them in the face all along.

"When people pray, does it work?" he asked.

Moynihan lifted his head and looked at him with undisguised surprise for a few seconds. "Well, now, there's a question that I wasn't expecting from one the likes of yourself," he declared.

"They do it all over, and they have been for thousands of years," Kopeksky went on. "That's enough to say to me that there could be something to it."

" 'Twould be a fine way I'd be wasting my life if there wasn't," Moynihan commented.

"But is there really anybody on the other end of the line?" Kopeksky persisted. "Or is it something that you trigger inside yourself?"

The tea arrived. Moynihan stroked his chin and regarded Kopeksky long and thoughtfully while Ann arranged cups and saucers, milk jug, and a sugar bowl on a side table between the two chairs, along with a silver pot covered by a padded cozy. Then she retired, closing the door again. Moynihan leaned over to pick up the pot and poured for both of them. "The tea goes in first. Then you can add enough milk to make it whatever strength you fancy. I just take a splash meself, with no more than half a spoon of sugar so you don't lose the flavor of the tea. 'Tis no good at all unless the spoon can stand up in it, in my opinion."

Kopeksky followed his example and tried a sip. It was hot, strong, and even the small drop filled his mouth with a taste that made everything he'd tried before insipid. "Not bad," he pronounced. "I could get used to this."

"I'll let you have a small box to take home and experiment with," Moynihan said. He stared into the fire, set his own cup down, and looked across at

Kopeksky again. "Getting back to your question, how many times did Christ tell us that God's kingdom is within? But that's the one place where people refuse to look. The Buddha told them to reject external ministrations as the means of deliverance and find their own eightfold way to proper thought. Confucius taught inner integrity as the only basis for a moral society." He made a brief openhanded gesture. "The one thing that all the true religions of the world have ever said is the same. But people insist on demanding outside powers to help them. Therefore that's what we must be." Frank and direct, with no beating about the bush. It was also an assessment of Kopeksky and a statement of presumption that Kopeksky understood. The priest wrinkled his nose and rubbed it with a knuckle. "It's a strange kind of question to be coming from a policeman, if you don't mind me saying so."

Which was as good a way as any of asking what this was all about. Kopeksky nodded, having expected it. "This business that's jumbling up time all over the city. Some scientists have got a theory that it could be due to the activities of some kind of other intelligences, in a dimension that we don't interact with directly." He deliberately avoided any mention of "stealing." For one thing, Grauss had no evidence to warrant such an interpretation; for another, this whole thing was zany enough already without straining Moynihan's credulity further. Moynihan, however, accepted the suggestion with surprising matter-of-factness and had evidently seen where Kopeksky's line of thinking was leading.

"A strange matter to be involving people like yourselves in," Moynihan remarked. "Are these intelligences considered to be violating the law?"

"You know how it is with bureaucrats."

Moynihan sighed and inclined his head. "I'm

afraid that my limited abilities are only good for trying to communicate something to members of our own species in these familiar dimensions," he said. "The Church doesn't presume to extend its dictates to other beings in other realities that it has no knowledge of. Apparently the same notions of self-restraint don't apply to secular legislators. Ah, well . . ." He shook his head regretfully. "I'm sorry, Mr. Kopeksky, but I don't think I can supply what you're looking for."

Kopeksky had already concluded as much. But it was something to have been listened to and taken seriously. He realized that without its feelings the least bit unnatural, he had divulged more to Moynihan than to anyone else he had spoken to since the thing began. Maybe there was more to priests than he had realized, he thought to himself. They talked more about the bizarre behavior of the city's clocks over a second cup of tea and were equally lost for the beginnings of an idea of what could be done about it. Finally Kopeksky rose and announced that he had to be on his way. As had by now became habit, he compared his watch with the clock on the mantelpiece again. The two were still in agreement. He added a note of the fact to the other figures that he had been collecting since the previous morning, then left.

The first thing he encountered on emerging was an electronics shop that had managed to get three channels showing on the TVs in the window, all showing gabbling heads and different times. As he walked on, he thought back to the place that he had just left, with its calm, dependability, and image of unpretentious integrity. An island of sanity in a world that was coming closer to literally not knowing what day it was. Just as Moynihan had said.

00:06

When Kopeksky got back, the Bureau had just updated itself from 3:27 local to 4:00 P.M. EST. It had thus lost thirty-three minutes in the process, and everyone was flying around in a frenzy. Wade didn't have time to talk to anybody, nothing in the Day Room was making any sense, and Deena was still out chasing leads. He went on up to their office on the twelfth floor, got himself a coffee, and sat down at his desk to see once more if he could make anything out of the figures that he had been gathering.

The most affected locations, as measured by the rate at which their time fell behind the standard being maintained outside the area, seemed to be the telephone exchanges, TV centers, several of the larger data-processing bureaus, the City University computer center on the West Side, an automated machining plant in Queens, and the physics faculty at Columbia University. And at all of them the situation had been getting worse over the last two days, with two exceptions that stood out notably: the improvement at JFK since it ceased operating; and the reduced lag that the telephone exchanges experienced during the nights.

Kopeksky spread the sheets of paper out and stared at them, clasping his coffee mug in front of him between the fingers of both hands. The only thing that came to mind immediately about the places he had flagged with asterisks was that they were all fairly heavy users of computer systems of some kind or another. . . . Or were they? Did TV centers do much computing? He didn't know. And the power companies were high in the ranking there, but he wasn't sure how much computing went on in connection with generating electricity. Something to check. He wrote the word *Computers?* in large letters on his scratch pad and circled it in red, then sat for a while contemplating it, waiting for it to tell him something. It didn't . . . but there had to be something significant in the fact that the two cases he knew about of the trend reversing had both occurred after a substantial drop in activity.

He picked up the phone and called JFK International, hitting lucky by getting through on the second try. A couple of minutes later he was through to a Marty Fasseroe, the engineer in charge of maintenance for most of the airport's computer facilities. Kopeksky explained who he was, why he was calling, and obtained some more figures for his collection from the records in Fasseroe's log. Then he asked, "Is the problem connected with the computers somehow? Have they been acting up in any way?"

There was a pause, indicating that Kopeksky had

scored a hit on something. Then Fasseroe replied, "Not what you'd call acting up, exactly. But . . ."

"There is something that's not right?" Kopeksky prompted.

"The timings and disk synchs are all out. It's as if the internal clocks are even more screwed up than what's going on outside. Programs run correctly, but they take longer than they should—sometimes as much as twenty-five percent. At least, that's how it was when we were trying to run normally. Since we suspended operations, it's down to about five, maybe six percent."

"Are you shut down completely? The computers, I mean?"

"Not completely. We're still running some monitoring and logging operations. But we don't have any traffic to deal with now, and regional ATC is being handled outside the affected area. So all the heavy stuff is down, yes."

Kopeksky added the information to his notes. "Okay," he pronounced. And then, routinely, "Anything else unusual?"

"Well, yeah, there was one other funny thing—up until early yesterday, that is. Inside the machines . . ."

"You mean the computers?"

"Yes. In the processor and memory cabinets—the guts of where it all happens—for a while we were getting this kind of . . . red haze. Everything in there turned red . . . you know, like in a photographer's dark room. And when you stuck a flashlight in there to look, the light from that turned red too. Nobody here ever saw anything like it."

"But it's not there now?"

"No. It went away soon after we reverted to

standby operations. I know I've never seen anything like it before."

"Well, thanks, Mr. Fasseroe. It's been a big help. If anything else strange happens, would you let me know?"

"Sure, I'd be happy to."

Kopeksky gave his direct number and hung up. Then he tried calling Fasseroe's counterparts at Newark and La Guardia to see if the patterns they had experienced there were in any way similar, but he was unable to get through in either case. He did get an operator at the local Manhattan exchange, however, who, after an initially rancorous response since she was harassed and not in a mood for dealing with kooks and their questions that day, put him through to a supervisor at the engineering section. Kopeksky asked his by now routine questions about what time standard the company was using, how often they reset to it, and how many minutes they drifted in the meantime. It turned out that currently the exchange computers were running slow by about twenty-three percent. Then he said, "Just one more thing. Out of curiosity, is there anything unusual going on inside the boxes? Maybe things turning red in there—what could be described as a red light, or 'haze'?"

"How did you know about that?" the supervisor asked. He sounded suspicious.

"Just a hunch," Kopeksky replied. "JFK had it too, before they closed down. Nobody there knows what it was, either. Does it suggest anything to you?"

"One guy here thinks it's black holes. The radiation field generated from time falling into submicroscopic black holes. He's into some strange things, though—you know, science fiction and stuff."

"Does he have any ideas what to do about it?" Kopeksky asked.

"We don't know. He figured the whole world is going to disappear down the same drain, and got so drunk we had to send him home. I could give you his number, but I don't think it'd do you much good. He's out of it until tomorrow. Or we all go down the tubes. Whichever happens first."

"Thanks anyhow. Would you let me know if anything else unusual happens?"

Kopeksky spent the remainder of the afternoon compiling a list of further locations and calling them, including the Stock Exchange, Weather Bureau, computer centers at the major banks and several hospitals, and a number of scientific research centers. He found he could carry on into the evening past normal working hours because in many cases the clocks at the places he was calling were still indicating late afternoon. But when Kopeksky checked, the people there agreed with him that it was dark outside—which according to their clocks it shouldn't have been. Hence it seemed that even at the same location the time according to an artificial timekeeping device could be one thing while that given by the sun was another. When Kopeksky called down to the Day Room to check the situation at Bureau HQ itself, he was informed that the sun had been observed to set six minutes before the clocks that had been reset to EST less than an hour earlier said it should have done.

He sat back wearily and looked at the litter on his desk, which by now was beginning to resemble Deena's. Lots of numbers. Still no pattern to them. He didn't think like a computer. What he needed was a picture.

He went down to the library and checked out a

large-scale wall map of the New York area, then brought it back up and fixed it to the wall between his desk and Deena's. Then he called out for a pepperoni-salami pizza and salad to keep him going through the evening, rolled up his sleeves, and commenced the task of figuring out a system for turning his figures into some kind of a chart that would, hopefully, reveal something meaningful.

It was 9:25 according to his pocket windup when Deena called (but 9:21 by the digital watch on his other wrist, 9:02 by the Bureau clock on the wall, which had been reset to EST at 6:00 that evening, and 8:26 according to the channel showing on the portable TV that he'd set up in a corner of the office, which had just been restored after a retuning of the transmitter). Her usual routine for getting hold of him in the evening was to call first his apartment, followed by his three favorite neighborhood restaurant-bars. That she had gone on to try the office next said that it was something urgent.

"The astronomers couldn't really help. But I think I've found a scientist that you ought to talk to," she told Kopeksky when he answered.

"You mean there's a sane one?" he said.

"Well, he talks English and he seems to make sense."

"Where are you? And what the hell are you doing still out knocking on doors at this time? Did your landlady throw you out or something?"

"I'm at a place called Scicomp—that's short for Scientific Computing Institute. It's a fairly new place on the East Side, just as you come off the Queensboro Bridge. It's computer city in here. They take on research contracts for all kinds of scientific work that needs big computing—you know, the heavy stuff.

They're into, oh"—Kopeksky could picture her delving into a pile of notes while she wedged the phone on a shoulder—"things like cosmology, particle physics, big economic models, engineering simulations, reality modeling. . . . The place is packed with specialized equipment that you don't see everywhere: Crays, Connection Machines, pipeline processors, super graphics."

Whatever they were. "Okay, I get the idea," Kopeksky said. "So what gives?"

"Well, I don't know how many words Eskimos have for 'panic,' but that's what it is here. We thought that the phone exchanges and TV centers were being hit the hardest, but this place is even worse. What time do you have back there right now, Joe?"

Kopeksky looked at his windup again. "Nine twenty-six."

"Right. And I just called NBC to check there. They're showing 8:30." That was close enough to the channel showing on Kopeksky's TV, which was from a different network.

"Okay," he acknowledged.

"But here inside Scicomp it's only 7:21. We're over an hour behind the networks, even. I haven't come across anywhere like this. Everything's going crazy here."

"How did you find out about it?"

"It was a lead I got from somebody I talked to at an IBM site I was at. The computer people around town seem to be getting a better feel for the pattern of whatever's going on. It looks like a lot of installations are affected. And the airports and the phone companies use them a lot. I'm beginning to think that this whole thing might have something to do with computers somehow."

Which was the direction that Kopeksky's thinking had been heading. "So who's this guy I should talk to?" he asked.

"His name is Dr. Graham Erringer. He's a physician here, running simulations of, what was it? . . . Oh, yes, here we are. *Electromagnetic Pinch Filaments in the Pregravitational Plasma Universe.*" Deena paused. "Er, I guess that's what he does," she said to fill the silence that greeted her from the other end of the line.

"And he knows what's going on?" Kopeksky said finally.

"He's intrigued by what Grauss had to say, anyhow. And the engineers here have downed the machine he was working on, so he's got plenty of time now. Like I said, he seems to make sense. I think we should talk to him, Joe."

"Okay, see if you can set something up here at the Bureau for first thing tomorrow morning. . . . Oh, and Deena?"

"Yes?"

"Ask them if they've been finding anything unusual inside them computers, willya—maybe like a red light, or a funny red hazy effect."

Deena's voice took on a note of surprise. "Why, yes, they have! We were just talking about it. That was why they stopped Erringer's machine. How did you know about that?"

"Hey, kid," Kopeksky said, leaning back in his chair and feeling pleased, "don't think you're the only genius in the Bureau. I know a little bit about researching cases too, you know."

After he hung up, Kopeksky stared at the figures that he had noted and asked himself why things should be in a panic where Deena was, where it was still only 7:21. On the face of it, oughtn't she to have *more* time available, not less? It was all a case of whose time they decided was correct, he supposed. As far as he was concerned it was late evening, and he had accomplished a lot. If they agreed that his time was correct—in other words that the aliens had been taking time from Scicomp, where Deena was, which was what the theory said—then she would have to adjust her clock to his, which meant she'd suddenly find that it was half after nine with a whole chunk of the evening gone and nothing to show for it. If, on the other hand, he were to adjust to her, he'd find himself back with a whole evening ahead, but with his work still done. Yes, he told himself, when you got around to looking at it that way, that part of it did seem to add up.

But why should the aliens take time from there rather than time from someplace else? Why would they prefer a TV network's time to the Bureau's time, say . . . but less so at night? All very strange. Kopeksky poured himself another coffee and studied the figures again. He had begun marking them on a transparent overlay covering the map on the wall. He hoped that Dr. Erringer would be able to make more out of what they meant than Kopeksky could just at this moment.

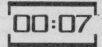

The next morning there was a note from Ellis Wade on Kopeksky's desk, along with a copy of a fax from Grauss, who was apparently now at the Fermi National Accelerator Laboratory near Chicago. From what Kopeksky could make of it, Grauss had come up with a theory that the energy consumed in particle-pair creations could somehow be used to send signals to the aliens who were helping themselves to New York's time. The powers in Washington had considered anything worth a try and sent Grauss to Fermilab to guide the scientists there in setting up a suitable experiment. There was also an apologetic message from Dr. Erringer, saying that he would be late. Kopeksky showed Deena the chart that he had been developing and let her take over the task of adding the remaining figures, while he went up to the fifteenth floor to see what more Wade could tell him about the latest from Grauss.

He found Wade sitting dazedly at his desk, and his secretary, Ruth, cowering inarticulately in a corner while a lean, hawk-faced man in a black suit delivered a harangue, at the same time stabbing a finger at an open Bible that he was holding. With him were two women, also in black, their hair tied up in buns and held by white mesh bonnets.

"Can you not see that this is a repeat of the warning that was given to us with Babel? Man built him a tower, thinking that it could gain him the heavens, but God confused him with many tongues. And now, again, we seek machines to go where only the righteous may ascend, and God confuses us with many times. It was foretold here in Matthew, 'Can ye not discern the signs of *the times*?' "

"Who are they?" Kopeksky muttered at Ruth from the door.

"How do I know?" she returned desperately. "What are they even doing in the building?"

The man's voice reverberated stridently across the office. "Hear the revelation of St. John: 'The devil is come down unto you, having great wrath, because he knoweth that he hath but a short *time*.' "

Then Wade noticed for the first time that Kopeksky was there. A look of relief flooded into his face and his mouth started to open. Kopeksky felt for the doorknob behind him and backed out, raising a hand protectively. "Sorry, Ellis. I just remembered something downstairs that can't wait. Talk to you later when you're not so busy, huh?" He walked away rapidly, declining to wait for an elevator and taking the stairs instead.

Opinions around the water fountain were that the

time-dilation anomaly would spread around the world within a month, and the only way out would be a reversion to preindustrial living. The Bureau's Finance and Commerce section was inundated with a rash of insurance scams involving the advance purchase of cover in one part of the city against incidents that had already happened in another, and international stock trading was in chaos.

By the time Kopeksky got back to his own office Erringer had arrived and was showing a lot of interest in the chart. Except that it was now "charts": Erringer and Deena had moved a table over to the wall below the map and were busy with colored marking pens, copying the figures from Kopeksky's original onto a series of separate overlays.

"What's this?" Kopeksky asked them as he ambled in.

Deena turned to gesture but knocked a stack of papers off the corner of the table. "It's Graham's suggestion," she said over her shoulder as she stooped to collect them. "We're grouping the data into twelve-hour time frames. The way the pattern changes might tell us something."

"Not a bad idea," Kopeksky agreed. A similar thought had occurred to him the night before, but it had been too late then to do anything about it.

"Oh." Deena straightened up and put the papers on her desk. "This is Graham Erringer that I mentioned, from Scicomp. Dr. Erringer, that is . . . And this is Joe Kopeksky."

The two men shook hands. Erringer was tall and athletically built, with a ruddy, healthy complexion, shaggy blond hair, and relaxed features that smiled easily. Kopeksky guessed him to be around thirty-five. He was wearing a tan sport jacket with a patterned V-neck sweater and light blue open-necked shirt.

"I'm sorry I was late, Mr. Kopeksky," he said. "We had another crisis this morning. And we're constantly running out of time over there—but you already know that, of course."

"It's happening all over," Kopeksky said.

Erringer turned to look at the wall map again. "This is very interesting. It's the first time I've seen a systematic compilation of the whole picture." He raised a hand briefly. "I hope you don't mind my intruding like this. Sorting the data by time seemed the obvious next step, and I couldn't contain my curiosity. We haven't interfered with your original."

"That's okay," Kopeksky said. "It's the next thing I was thinking of trying, anyhow."

Erringer gestured at the new charts that Deena was working on. "The points are still a bit thin, but it's already evident that there's a pattern there. We're adding in some more figures that I brought with me, mainly pertaining to computer installations."

"Do you figure this whole thing has got something to do with computers?" Kopeksky asked.

"Possibly. Sites with large facilities certainly seem to show longer time lags," Erringer replied.

"Like Scicomp."

"One of the largest so far."

"And you had that funny red haze inside the boxes there."

"Yes," Erringer said. "That was why the engineers shut down the machine I was using—to investigate the haze. Other installations have been reporting the same thing, as I presume you already know. That must be how you came to be aware of it."

Kopeksky nodded. "Does anyone have any idea what it is?"

Erringer turned to sit against the edge of the table below the map. "From the measurements I've seen, the time loss isn't simply one number that applies to the whole of a place"—he motioned with an arm at the room around them—"such as this building. The rates can be different, even at two points quite close to each other, say two different kinds of clocks in the same room."

That was what Kopeksky himself had observed with his two watches, and from the lack of correlations between sunset times and clock times at various locations. He nodded.

Erringer went on, "The greatest lags of all seem to occur inside the cabinets of large processor and memory arrays—in some cases we've looked at, more than thirty-five percent. But at the same time, the clocks in the room outside the cabinets might be losing at only, say, six or seven percent." Erringer gave an apologetic smile, as if for something too farfetched to treat seriously. "Well, what it looks like to me is a localized red shift. Time inside the cubicle is slowing down sufficiently to produce a visible lengthening of the wavelengths of the light in there. Are you familiar with red shift?"

"Losing time is effectively the same as saying it's running slower," Deena threw in from where she was tiptoed on a chair, fixing the first of the revised overlays onto the map. "When time runs slower, light gets redder. Colors are due to frequencies, which depend on time. So when it changes, they all shift."

"Quite," Erringer said, nodding.

Kopeksky thought for a moment. "So is that why the radio and TV channels keep having to be retuned?"

Erringer nodded again. "Exactly."

They were getting some information at last, even if it didn't explain everything yet. Might as well throw everything in while they were at it, Kopeksky decided. "So what about this guy Grauss's idea that we've got aliens stealing it?" he said. "Does that make sense to you?"

Erringer gave another apologetic smile and hesitated. "I don't quite see the factual support that says just because it seems to be disappearing, someone is taking it deliberately," he replied. "With all due respect to a professional colleague, my answer would be—"

The phone rang.

"Excuse me," Kopeksky muttered, picking it up. Then, louder, "This is Kopeksky."

"Joe, Harry here in the Day Room. We've got a visitor down here asking for you: a Father Moynihan. Want me to send him up?"

Kopeksky's eyebrows lifted in surprise. "Sure. I'll meet him at the elevators."

"He's on his way."

"Who is it?" Deena asked from where she was still standing on the chair. She let a corner of the transparency slip before it was pinned and almost lost her balance trying to catch it. Erringer stepped in deftly and saved the situation.

"The priest from yesterday," Kopeksky told her.

"What does he want?"

"Good question. You okay?"

"Sure." Deena stepped back down to the floor, kicking a box of thumbtacks off the chair in the process.

"Back in a few minutes," Kopeksky said.

So Erringer thought that Grauss was rushing into a blind alley, Kopeksky thought as he walked out into the corridor of banging doors and scurrying figures. He wondered how much luck Grauss would have persuading the Fermilab scientists to go along with his experiment if they felt the same way.

Moynihan was in uniform this time, with a black raincoat, white dog collar, and carrying a furled umbrella. In his other hand he was carrying a leather bag from which he produced a package in white plastic wrapping. "I'm after forgetting to give you the tea that I promised yesterday," he explained. "It so happened that I was passing this way, so I thought I might as well drop it in. Punjana—one of me favorites."

"Er, thanks." Kopeksky took the package. "Tea first. Half a spoon of sugar, just a splash of milk. Right?"

"Grand man, you've got it. Oh, and I wondered if you might be interested in these." Moynihan dug into the bag and began pulling out books two or three at a time. "I picked out some works on mystical experiences. I can't be sure that what I said about our own product offering applies to all brands, you understand. For all I know, there might be others who've stumbled on things that could point a way to contacting these aliens of yours. Anyhow, for what help they might be, you're welcome to borrow them."

"We'll check it out, anyway," Kopeksky said, taking the books. After the trouble that the priest had gone to, he didn't want to say that the case for aliens appeared to be receding.

"And I remembered how interested you were that the clocks at St. Vitus agreed with that silver pocket watch that you were carrying, and I saw how you were noting down the times of everything," Moynihan went on, feeling inside the bag again. "So I did a little bit of extra research for you meself, that I thought might be useful." He drew out a black notebook and opened it to reveal several columns of neatly penned numbers. "These are the corresponding figures for the rest of our churches and other establishments around and about. It was a great excuse to call all me colleagues last night and catch up on the gossip."

Kopeksky grinned appreciatively. "You went to a lot of trouble."

"Ah, not at all, at all, at all."

Nevertheless, Kopeksky felt that he could hardly just say thanks and send Moynihan on his way—at least, not without offering a cup of tea. "Everything helps," he acknowledged. "How would you like to see what we're doing with it?"

"Well, if it wouldn't be interrupting the good work . . . ?"

"Nah, that's okay. The office is this way." They began walking back along the corridor. Nobody had said anything about this business being secret, Kopeksky reflected. Anyhow, if the official aim was to try to attract the attention of aliens who didn't even know that humanity existed, how could secrecy be an issue?

They joined Deena and Erringer in the office. Kopeksky introduced Moynihan and explained what was going on. Erringer accepted Moynihan's notebook eagerly and began transferring the figures from it to the several overlays now covering the map, one for each half-day period for the last two and a half days. "This is interesting," Erringer commented. "They're all like oases in the middle of it. Hardly affected at all."

"Islands of sanity," Moynihan said. "Aren't I after telling you the same thing yesterday?"

"True," Kopeksky agreed.

"And then there are these other kinds of islands

where we have things going to the other extreme, such as at Scicomp," Erringer said, pointing. "Where the time lags are greatest. Look—again, distinctly localized."

"Ah." Moynihan stepped forward to peer at the chart with interest.

"A lot of them seem to be places that have got big computers," Kopeksky commented.

"Is that a fact?" Moynihan lifted the top overlay to study the one beneath, and then the next one beneath that.

"Actually, I think it might not be quite as simple as that," Erringer cautioned. "See here, the TV centers don't use what you'd call excessive computing, but they're high up there. Same with the phone exchanges—they're scattered around a lot, not as big as you might think. Same thing with the utilities."

"What, then?" Kopeksky asked him.

"It looks as if it has something to do with electrical activity, which of course includes computers," Erringer said. "But exactly what, at this stage it's difficult to say. We'd need to analyze what's going on at these high-dilation centers and see what kind of correlations we get." He rubbed his chin between thumb and forefinger and ran his eye over the map again. "Regular patterns of fast switching seem to come into it. But I think it has to do with power densities as well. . . . Maybe some kind of more complex relationship that involves the two."

"What can you make out of that?" Deena asked him.

"Right at this moment, not a hell of a lot more than that," Erringer confessed.

Moynihan had gone back to the earliest of the charts and was turning slowly through the sequence again, studying each intently and muttering an occasional "Ah, yes" and "There we are" to himself. The others fell silent and waited curiously. Finally Moynihan stepped back and looked at them.

"Now, I don't know too much meself about computers and the like, you understand," he said. "But I do know a little about the characteristic spreading pattern of an epidemic when I see one. Look, there are your primary infection sources there, there, and here. And you can see the secondary centers and the growth over the ensuing two days. The spread has stopped at the airports following the closures." Moynihan made an openhanded gesture that said they could make what they liked out of it, but those were the facts. "Never mind aliens," he said. "It's bugs ye should be looking for, if you want my opinion on the matter."

"Bugs? You mean software bugs are real?" Deena shook her head hopelessly. "This is getting insaner."

Before anyone could say more, the phone rang again. This time Deena answered. "It's for you," she said, holding the phone out to Erringer. "Somebody from Scicomp."

He took the phone. His expression grew serious as he listened. Finally he said, "I'll be right back," and hung up.

Nobody bothered asking the obvious. "Things are getting worse back there," Erringer told them. "The red haze is spreading out into the building. Also they're finding problems with the structure all of a sudden. We may have to close the place down entirely, which would be ruinous. I have to get back and see what we can do."

"Mind if I come along?" Kopeksky said.

"Sure, if you want. Do you have any ideas?"

"No."

"You'd better carry on with the map, now that it looks like we might be getting somewhere," Kopeksky said to Deena. "Get some help from one of the techs downstairs—somebody who knows about, what was it? . . ." He looked at Erringer. "Fast electrical switching patterns and power densities? That was what you said, right?"

"Right." Erringer nodded.

"Will do," Deena confirmed.

"And I have to be heading on me way," Moynihan said. "I'm glad I was able to help."

"Maybe more than you think," Kopeksky answered. "Sorry to have to break it up like this. We didn't even get to make any tea."

"Perhaps another time," Moynihan said, checking that he had his bag and his umbrella. "My turn to take the rain check, I gather."

Kopeksky looked at Erringer again. "Anything else, Doc?"

"No. I guess that's it."

"Then let's go."

The cabs they tried hailing were all full and burning rubber—an all-yellow Indianapolis 500. But then one screeched to a stop right in front of Bureau HQ to disgorge a fat man in a fawn coat who practically threw a twenty at the cabbie and scampered away into the entrance next door without stopping to wait for change. "They're doing it all over." The cabbie chuckled, tucking the bill away as Kopeksky climbed in. "Whatever's going on in this city, it's one of the best things that ever happened. Your pleasure, gentlemen?" Erringer gave the address and got in beside Kopeksky.

"So what are pinch filaments in the pregravitational universe?" Kopeksky asked as the cab moved off.

"You don't forget much," Erringer said. He made it a compliment.

"Aw, in this job you're pestering people all the time with questions," Kopeksky replied. "It doesn't help make friends if you have to keep asking them over again."

"What got you into this line of work?"

"I never could stay away from trouble. So I figured that if I was going to be around it anyway, I might as well get paid for it."

Erringer nodded. "That makes sense, I guess."

They edged out onto Ninth and were almost hit by a Toyota van running the red light. "So what are these filaments?" Kopeksky asked again.

"Oh . . . basically we're pretty certain now that what people have been told for years about the Big Bang origin of the universe is all wrong. It never happened. There isn't enough mass for gravity to have formed galaxies in the fifteen billion years since the universe is supposed to have formed, and there are larger-scale structures out there that go back way, way further than that. My line of work involves compression of an initially diffuse, primordial plasma medium into extended filaments by electromagnetic forces, which are trillions of times stronger than gravity. Gravitational collapse only came later."

"Oh," Kopeksky said.

"It's basically an optimistic view, because it leads to a picture of an evolving universe, not one that's degenerating to a heat death. In fact, just the opposite."

"You mean it's winding up, not running down?" Kopeksky said. Despite the technicalities, he'd heard enough bits of the subject to follow the essentials of what Erringer was saying.

"Exactly. We're evolving away from equilibrium, creating bigger temperature differences that increase energy flows. Extrapolation of the second law to a universal scale simply isn't valid." Erringer waited a couple of seconds, then decided it was time to change the subject. "I imagine you must meet all kinds of people," he said, switching back to Kopeksky's work again.

"You can say that again. Most of them are mean, dumb, or crazy. But there are a few okay ones too, who make up for it."

"That priest who was back at the office," Erringer said. "Father Moynihan. He seems like an interesting person."

"Oh, sure. You don't get a lot like that."

"How does he come to know so much about diseases?"

"He worked in Africa years ago. Medical missionary. His specialty was diseases you get from bugs. Says he still keeps bugs in his basement today, kinda like a hobby."

"Interesting." There was another short pause. Kopeksky pretended not to notice Erringer's quick glance sideways at him. "That woman you work with, er . . ."

"Deena?"

"Right. She's quite an interesting person too. Very intelligent, compared to many that you meet. She seems to know something about practically everything."

"Deena's a good partner," Kopeksky said. "We've worked together for four years. I wouldn't trade."

"Is she, er, you know, married . . . anything like

that?" Erringer tried with abysmal lack of success to make his voice nonchalant.

Kopeksky's eyebrows shot upward. "No, nothing like that," he replied. "I've never known a freer spirit." Was he detecting some personal attraction here?

" 'Free spirit,' " Erringer repeated, sitting back. "Yes, that's a good way to put it. She does have this charming spontaneity about her, don't you think?"

Kopeksky turned his face away to gaze out at the perpetual still-life study of Manhattan's crosstown traffic. Charming spontaneity. He'd never heard it put that way before. "Yep, I guess you could call it that," he agreed. His face split into a craggy smirk. Maybe Erringer was right, and the universe wasn't such a bad place after all.

The scene outside the Scientific Computing Institute on East Fifty-ninth Street had the look of a national emergency. Several fire trucks with uncoiled hoses and ladders extended were drawn up in front of the building, but their crews stood around uncertainly since there wasn't any fire to tackle. They had no doubt been called because of the eerie red glow showing through several of the second- and third-floor windows, Kopeksky guessed as he and Erringer got out of the cab. There were also police cruisers parked haphazardly all over the street, which had been closed for two blocks, and a couple of military vehicles from which soldiers in National Guard uniforms were unloading boxes and reels of cable. On the far side, a crowd of what Kopeksky took to be Scicomp employees were standing watching, having presumably been evacuated from the building.

Kopeksky followed Erringer over to some people who looked like management, talking and gesticulating with a group of police and Guard officers. While Erringer hurried forward to join them, Kopeksky stood back and ran an eye over the Scicomp Building again. He could see the fluorescent tubes on the ceilings in the rooms that seemed to be affected the most. The light that they were emitting was red, not the normal white. And through the large glass doors of the entrance at ground level he could see that the light in the reception area was also tinted, but not to the same degree as higher up. There was something odd about the figures visible in there—something about the way they moved. Their postures and attitudes as they gestured to and fro at each other, went in and out of doors, and crossed the vestibule floor, all told of haste and agitation inside; but there was a strange floating quality to the way they went about it all, as if the whole scene were curiously unreal. And then Kopeksky realized why: The slow-down factor of time in there had grown big enough to see. The people that he was looking at were literally living in a different time.

He moved over to one of the patrolmen standing nearby and flashed his ID. "Kopeksky, City Bureau. What's the score here?"

"I'm not too sure," the patrolman answered. "All I know is it's a big computer center of some kind. From what I hear of it, the time glitches that have been happening all over really went wild here. That's what's making the spooky red up there."

"Why the army?"

"None of the phones are working. They're running field sets inside." The cop shook his head wonderingly. "It's time to go home, man. This doesn't happen in Wyoming."

Then Erringer came back over, accompanied by a man in a checked overcoat. Erringer introduced him as Chuck Milliken, an engineer from a firm of architectural consultants who had been involved with the construction of the building. They had been called in to help investigate the structural problems that were the latest thing to have been reported. The problems seemed to be appearing in the places where the time dilation was greatest.

"It's worst down in the basement, where we've got a trio of new supercomputers hooked together doing comprehensive climatic modeling," Erringer told Kopeksky. "That was where the haze began spreading first, and then all the disk drives started seizing up. External communications are out all over the building. The Guard are trying army field telephones with local frequency shifters to talk to the outside—in case it gets worse at other places too, and they have to set up an emergency net for the whole city. Anyhow, let's go inside and take a look."

"You're sure it's healthy in there?" Kopeksky asked dubiously.

Erringer managed a grin despite the strain of the moment. "Oh, sure. The effect is purely perceptual. Come on, follow me."

They crossed the street, and the policemen standing a short distance back from the entrance parted to let them through. As the three approached the glass doors, the light inside gradually lost its pinkish hue and the moving figures seemed to quicken to a more natural pace, until, as Erringer opened the door, and Kopeksky and Milliken followed him through, everything became normal. Around them people were hurrying about, yelling, waving, running up and down the stairwell. On one side of them, a soldier wearing a headset was turning knobs on a communications box set up on the reception desk, from which a voice was gabbling unintelligibly, sounding like one of the Chipmunks. Beside him, another soldier was talking into a hand mike. "Slow it down, slow it down, for chrissakes! We can't make out what you're talkin' about." Kopeksky stopped and looked back the way they had come. Now everything in the street outside looked strangely cold and blue. And the people out there were strutting about with stiff, jerky movements reminiscent of old-time movies. Kopeksky shook his head, then turned to follow the others.

They used the stairs, since the elevators were either out of commission or shut down as a precaution. The basement area presented a repeat of the experience upstairs, appearing reddened as they came out from the stairway, then changing to normal coloring as they moved into it. The place was typical of the larger computer setups that Kopeksky had seen, although glitzier and more elaborate than most: rows of metal cubicles with consoles and lights, lots of screens and keyboards, thick carpeting and glass-walled offices. Erringer went over to talk to some technicians who had opened up several of the cubicles and were probing inside with tools and test instruments, manuals lying open on the floor and countertops around them. The insides of the units they were working on, Kopeksky could see, were noticeably red. That meant red with respect to the normal-looking room that they were in, which he already knew was itself red to the world outside. He gave up trying to visualize what it all meant. Maybe it was time to move to Wyoming.

In another area, by a door leading through to another part of the installation, several of the electronics units had been pushed back against a wall, and a part of the false floor taken up to expose the tangles of cables beneath. Two men were examining the concrete beams and steel ties of the underlying structure, and cutting off pieces of the floor supports.

"Those have to be your guys," Kopeksky said, turning to Milliken. "What kind of problems are you finding, exactly?"

The engineer waved toward one of the cabinets that had been moved back. "Damnedest thing. The floor gave way underneath a heavy mass-storage unit, right there. There just isn't any way that should be able to happen. The metal under it just gave out. It's crazy. This building's practically brand-new."

"Did it use any new kind of material or some new wonder technique?" Kopeksky asked.

"Nope. It's all the same as everybody's been using for years. Doesn't make a scrap of sense."

"What about upstairs, where the red fuzz is inside the windows? Is there anything up there too?"

"There's a measurable sag in a couple of the floors, all right. That's why we moved most of the people out. If the foundations are affected too, we could be in real trouble." Milliken nodded to indicate the two men working under the floor. "Let's go see how Bill and Rick are doing." Kopeksky followed him over. "What's the news on the floor pillars?" Milliken inquired.

One of the two held up a piece of metal tube about eighteen inches long. It was buckled and misshapen, the material itself being at the same time swollen in a strange kind of way that didn't happen with metals. "If it was wood, I'd say we had a bad case of dry rot," the man said. "It's got no strength. We'll take some samples for testing, but it looks to me like the whole grain structure is disrupted." Kopeksky took the piece out of curiosity and examined it. It reminded him of bomb fragments that he had seen from time to time.

"What could cause it, Rick?" Milliken asked the other engineer.

"Beats the hell outta me."

"What about the foundation structure?"

The first engineer, who had to be Bill, selected a piece from a collection of concrete samples detached by drilling and chiseling and showed it. "This doesn't feel right, Chuck," he said. "Here, try for yourself. Too grainy. It's like it was mixed with too high a sand content."

"But that's not true. It was top quality," Milliken objected.

"I know that. But something's changed it since. It has to be whatever's corroding the steel here too, but don't ask me what."

"If you asked me I'd say it was mice," Rick said. "Except mice don't eat that kind of cheese."

Milliken passed the sample to Kopeksky, at the same time talking to Bill. "Is the integrity of the whole structure threatened? Does this mean a total evacuation?"

"I don't know. Could be. We need to go down farther and do some checks at the parking level. But it doesn't look good to me."

Kopeksky saw that Erringer was looking around for him. "I'd better get back to the doc," he told Milliken. "Can I keep these?" He showed the samples that he was holding.

"Who's he?" Bill asked Milliken.

"Police. He's with one of the scientists who works here." Milliken nodded to Kopeksky. "Go ahead.

We've got plenty more of it around here." He looked around and picked up an empty plastic bag that was lying on top of some boxes. "You can put them in this."

"Thanks."

"Nice talking to ya."

Kopeksky threaded between a graphics plotter and a line printer to where Erringer was standing with the computer technicians. Erringer saw him approaching and gestured toward the opened cubicle. It was filled with stacks of the green fiberglass boards packed with things that looked like rectangular cockroaches. The redness that he had seen from across the room was just "there." It didn't seem to emanate from any discernible source but permeated the interior of the unit as a diffuse reddening.

Erringer saw Kopeksky looking at it. "It was more pronounced earlier," he said. "Apparently it's eased off since they shut this machine down."

"Like at the airports," Kopeksky said.

"Quite."

"It quits when the switching stops."

"So it seems . . . after a while, anyhow. And there's this." Erringer showed him a piece of precision-made, rotary machinery, consisting of a shaft mounted in a bearing assembly, with supporting plate and bearings. But it was no longer so precise. The once-gleaming metal surfaces had lost their sheen and become buckled and distorted. Parts that should have turned freely were locked solid. "From one of the disk units," Erringer said. "Totally seized up. It's the same with the cooling fans and motors too, and the printers. All the mechanical peripherals are wrecked. That's going to cost hundreds of thousands alone."

There were other parts taken from different units,

and some printed circuit cards from the worst-affected electronics cabinets, which were apparently also nonfunctional. The cards showed the kind of deformation that Kopeksky would have expected to see had they been in a fire, but without any scorching. He added a couple of them to his collection of items to take back.

Then two men whom Kopeksky recognized from the managers that Erringer had talked to on the sidewalk outside appeared from the stairwell, which now had a bluish tint, and drew Erringer aside. Kopeksky heard some talk about a pier cracking on the second floor and then they called Milliken over, who came across with the engineer named Bill. Meanwhile, a police officer with lots of braid and several lieutenants came out from the stairway and hovered. Kopeksky decided that this wasn't the time to be hanging around waiting to ask theoretical questions. He caught Erringer's attention long enough to say that he would be on his way, and for Erringer to let him know the news when he had a chance. Then he left via the blue-tinted stairs to the lobby and exited into the blue-tinted street that suddenly reverted to normal daylight again.

Kopeksky found a pay phone in a coffee shop down the block but was unable to get through to the Bureau since the exchanges were having more than the usual amount of trouble. He went back to one of the police cruisers to try via the radio, but the channels had all drifted out of tune. If this was typical of what was happening citywide, they weren't far away from a complete breakdown. He thrust his hands deep in his overcoat pockets and stood staring back across the street at the facade of the Scicomp Building. More people were being brought out onto the street, drifting lazily through the pink light inside the lobby and then snapping into life as they came through the doors.

Mice, one of the engineers had said. Except that mice don't eat machinery—or steel and concrete from the inside until a building suddenly starts to fall down. If it had been wood, the other engineer had said, they would have had a bad case of dry rot. Kopeksky turned the words over in his head. Mice. Buildings. Wood. Wooden buildings. Wooden buildings falling down . . .

Termites.

"It's bugs, ye should be looking for," Moynihan had told them. What did bugs that ate buildings have to do with time? Kopeksky frowned and went over the question again, trying to ask himself what, exactly, he meant by it. He wasn't sure, but an instinct told him that there was a convoluted connection somewhere. Whom to talk to? Erringer was unavailable for the time being, and there didn't seem to be a way to contact anyone at the Bureau. Which left only one person.

Kopeksky walked over to the cruiser again. "I need a ride to the Lower East Side," he told the driver. "It's a church near the Manhattan Bridge. I'll give you directions when we get down there." He climbed in and showed the plastic bag containing the samples that he had collected. "And after you drop me off, I want you to take these to the materials lab at City Bureau HQ. Ask for a guy named Jack Orelli. Tell him we need a report on the internal condition of this stuff. It's from the place where we've had the worst time lag so far, which means they drop whatever else they're doing and give it priority. Okay? Let's move."

The basement room of the presbytery at St. Vitus in the Fields was brightly lit with fluorescent tubes and whitewashed brick walls. A laboratory-type bench with sink, burner, and microscope ran along one side beneath shelves carrying an assortment of chemical glassware, jars, and bottles, and a biological specimen cabinet with glass doors took up most of the other. On a solidly built table in the corner opposite the door was a glass-walled tank three-quarters full of sandy soil with pieces of wood and wet cardboard scattered on the surface. Inside it, hundreds of orange-bodied, waxy-looking insects were scurrying in and out and about an egg-shaped structure of what looked like cemented clay, partly exposed to reveal its extraordinarily intricate construction. It was about the size of a pineapple standing on end and made up from top to bottom of rows of galleries and openings leading through to the inside, arranged in regular tiers like the floors of a building.

First fish, now bugs, Kopeksky thought to himself as he watched. "It looks like Grand Central at five-thirty," he commented.

"This is a species from the genus *Apicotermes*, found mainly in the Congo basin," Father Moynihan informed him. "The nests of termites include some remarkably complex structures that are without parallel in the animal kingdom. This particular kind is strictly subterranean. But as you're probably aware, there are others that build mounds above ground, sometimes to amazing heights. Some in Australia can top twenty feet. That would be about the same as ourselves putting up a building over a mile high."

"They don't have to worry about the elevators going out," Kopeksky said, peering closely through the tank wall. The termites appeared soft-bodied, with no trace of a hard outer shell. "I always thought of them as kinda like ants. They don't look like ants."

"At one time they were popularly referred to as white ants, but the term is incorrect," Moynihan said. "They're a completely separate order that evolved from an ancestral stock resembling modern roaches: the order Isoptera—as opposed to Hymenoptera, which are the bees, wasps, and ants."

"So are there lots of different kinds?"

"More than you'll find freckles on an Irish Boy Scout troop."

"What makes up an order? Different species?" Kopeksky asked.

Moynihan nodded. "There are estimated to be somewhere between two and three thousand of them. As a rule they exist in more rigidly structured societies than other social insects—necessary for food sharing to exchange the bacteria and symbiotic microorganisms that they have to have to digest the cellulose they live on." He leaned forward to peer into the tank alongside Kopeksky and pointed. "See those. They're some of the soldiers, which are interesting. Their heads and bodies are so thoroughly modified into weapons that they can neither feed themselves nor reproduce. A bit like some Irishmen that I've known in me time."

Kopeksky straightened up. "And these are the guys who can eat your house away until it falls down, right?"

"Well, not this particular variety," Moynihan said. "All of them eat wood, true, but most of the damage to property is caused by what are called the Kalotermitidae or dry-wood family."

"Whatever," Kopeksky said. "They chew up a bit at a time from here, from there, all spread out so you don't notice at first. And then one day all that stuff that you thought you had under you isn't there anymore, and holes start appearing all over your house."

Moynihan moved back from the tank and recited:

> *"Some primal termite knocked on wood*
> *And tasted it and found it good,*
> *And that is why your cousin May*
> *Fell through the parlor floor today."*

"You write poems about them too?" Kopeksky sounded surprised.

"Ogden Nash."

"Oh. Okay. . . . Anyhow, what we think of as a solid building material, they see as food."

Moynihan scratched the side of his nose, unsure why Kopeksky was dwelling on this. "Yes, I suppose you could put it like that," he agreed. "A rather odd way to think of it, if you don't mind me saying. I have the suspicion, now, that you're leading up to something."

Kopeksky turned fully to face him. "Father, how much do you know about these universes that are supposed to exist in other dimensions, like these scientists keep talking about?"

"And why would you be asking me that, now?"

"Would something in this universe—the one we're in—still look like the same kind of . . . 'substance' to somebody in one of the other universes?" Kopeksky rapped the top of the bench with a knuckle. "This, for instance. To us it's real stuff. Hard and solid. Could it look like a 'hole,' say, to one of these aliens—not something solid at all? . . . Or maybe something that's completely different from substance: something that doesn't take up any room at all, empty or solid?"

"This is a fine riddle you're getting me into now," Moynihan said, wrinkling his face and trying to follow.

Kopeksky came to the point that had been forming in his mind ever since he left Scicomp. "When you were at the Bureau this morning, you said that what we oughta be looking for is bugs." He waved vaguely at the glass tank beside them. "Now this might sound crazy, I know, but I figure you're pretty used to it. Could you have a situation where something that's solid stuff in one of these other universes comes across like time in ours? See what I mean? Then if they had some kind of bugs that ate it, then it would be just food to them, but making holes all over the place in our time—just like with the species that eat houses."

Moynihan stared at him in astonishment. "Bugs? Bugs that eat time?" he repeated.

Kopeksky shrugged and showed his palms. "I listened to what you said and to what the doc said, and I look at what's been going on. It's the only thing I can think of that fits with what we've got."

As Kopeksky had expected, Moynihan did not ridicule the suggestion out of hand but paused to give it some thought. "That's an unbelievable thing that you're asking me to believe now," he said at last.

"I'm not saying it's true," Kopeksky said. "I'm just asking if you think it's possible."

"Well, stranger things have happened under heaven than either you or I are capable of imagining," Moynihan answered.

"So it isn't impossible?"

"I'd be the last one to tell you that it was."

Kopeksky felt suitably encouraged and went on, "The part of it that I still don't get is the building starting to fall apart at Scicomp. Maybe the story gets more complicated, and some of what these bugs eat *does* still look like solid stuff in our universe. What do you think?"

Moynihan held up a warning hand. "Wait a second, now. Don't you be putting me in the position of venturing an opinion. This is your own theory, not mine. It's the scientists that we should be putting this kind of a question to."

"We?"

Moynihan looked mildly indignant. "Well, of course 'we.' Now that you've got me curiosity roused, you don't think you're going to keep me away from finding out what the answers are, do you?"

Kopeksky had no problem with that. He nodded. "That's fine by me."

Moynihan went on, "I'd suggest talking to that fella Erringer. He struck me as one of the few that you meet who's prepared to listen more than he wants to talk."

The first thing would be to see what kind of reception this got back at the Bureau, Kopeksky decided. If the things he'd seen so far were a preview of what the rest of the city was in for, they were going to need as much head start as they could get—assuming that somebody came up with a way of doing anything about the situation.

"Communications are shaky all over, so we probably won't be able to get in touch with him that way," he said. "Can you go to Scicomp up at Fifty-ninth and drag him out if you have to, then get him over to Bureau HQ? I'll go on there and brief whoever I can get hold of that's around. I'll meet you there in an hour. Ask for Ellis Wade's office. He's my chief there. And his boss is a guy named Langlon. I'll be with one of them."

"Very good."

They left the basement and went up to the hallway leading to the front door. "An hour," Moynihan repeated as they put on their coats. "What time do you have now, just to be sure?"

Kopeksky pulled out his silver watch and compared it with the old grandfather clock ticking sedately by the hat stand. To his surprise the pocket watch was reading six minutes behind. He showed it and looked at Moynihan inquiringly. The priest raised his eyebrows and shrugged in a way that said Kopeksky could make anything of it that he wanted. Kopeksky hesitated, then adjusted his watch to conform to Moynihan's clock. They left and walked together to the end of the block, then parted to head for their respective destinations.

* * *

By the time Kopeksky got back to the Bureau, reports were pouring in of rapidly mounting chaos everywhere. The phones were practically all out, since time-shift reddenings had begun appearing in the exchanges, and the operators were refusing to work there. Staffs were walking out at a number of other large computer sites for the same reason, and several more buildings had been evacuated because of structural deterioration. Two—a data services center on the West Side and a clearing house for one of the major banks off lower Broadway—had actually started collapsing into themselves. Thousands of people were fleeing the city, and the tunnels and bridges exiting Manhattan were jammed.

Kopeksky checked that the samples he had sent from Scicomp had reached the lab and were being worked on, then went up to his office on the twelfth floor. Deena had recruited the help of one of the electrical specialists from Technical Services to complete the wall chart, and they were examining the results when Kopeksky joined them. The tech was new to the department, and Kopeksky had seen him around but not gotten to know him. His name was Hasley, and he looked all engineer: crew cut and wearing a short-sleeved shirt with its pocket stuffed with pens, rule, and a calculator.

"It's mainly large computer sites, but there are other focuses as well," he said when Kopeksky questioned him. "The time dilation seems to correlate with some combination of fast, regular, electrical switching activity and local power density. Without a lot of detailed investigations and measurements, I couldn't be more specific than that."

"Pretty much what Graham guessed," Deena said. Hasley nodded. "I'd say he was right."

"That's good enough for now," Kopeksky said. "I think we may have a new angle on it." He went on to summarize the theory that he had put to Moynihan and Moynihan's reaction to it. He concluded, "Don't tell me it's straight out of the *Far Side*, because I already know that. Does anyone have anything better?"

Deena hadn't. "Well, it's different. I'll give it that" was all she could offer.

Hasley shook his head in bafflement. "Bugs in another dimension, eating time? Hell, I don't know. I'm just an electrical engineer, not a witch doctor."

"I think we should talk to Graham," Deena said.

"Definitely," Hasley agreed.

"Moynihan's gone to Scicomp to bring him over," Kopeksky told them. "They should be here anytime. Meanwhile we need to fill in Ellis, before they show up."

"Oh-oh," Deena said ominously.

"What's up?" Kopeksky asked, sensing a problem.

"Grauss is back. Apparently there was a hell of a row with those scientists that he went to see up in Chicago. They seem to think he's crazy. Ellis and the rest of the suits are tearing about all over the place upstairs. I don't think you're gonna get sense out of anybody up there today."

"We'll see," Kopeksky replied.

Arriving at Wade's office on
the fifteenth floor, they
found Ruth valiantly
holding back a roomful of people
all gabbling at once and waving
their arms in the air, and with a
Christmas tree of lights flashing on
her desk. Kopeksky managed to
extract that Wade had fled to yet
higher ramparts of the building,
muttered a few words of
encouragement to Ruth, and left
again with Deena and Hasley.

Wade and Grauss had holed up
in the office of Wade's boss, David
Langlon, on the sixteenth. Langlon
had been academy-trained to
believe in delegation and usually
left it to Wade to handle awkward
visitors. Hence, his secretary was
less experienced than Ruth in
protecting the inner sanctum, and
no match for an old hand, like
Kopeksky, at getting into places
where he wasn't wanted.

Langlon was sitting behind his

desk, and Wade was in a visitor's chair on the other side, both looking equally glassy-eyed, while Grauss stood facing them from the wall opposite, in front of a whiteboard covered in diagrams and mathematical hieroglyphics. The departmental procedure manuals had nothing to say about this kind of situation, and Langlon was too dazed to offer any resistance to Kopeksky's intrusion. Wade started to go through the motions of checking his subordinate, but Kopeksky circumvented him with practiced ease and went on to repeat his story.

A stupefied silence settled on the room like a fog blanket when Kopeksky had finished. Langlon and Wade looked at each other helplessly, and then, as if with one mind, turned their heads toward the scientist for salvation. Grauss was still standing motionless before the whiteboard, a red marker pen in one hand and his eyes popping like poached eggs behind his Coke-bottle lenses.

"Pugs!" he managed to choke out at last. "Serious issues are ve concerned mit on der breakthrough fringe porderlands of science, unt of pugs you are talkink us? Vass iss mit pugs? Vere kommen from, zese pugs?"

"He says you're a nut," Wade interpreted.

"Why am I a nut any more than him?" Kopeksky demanded indignantly. "What is there that says somebody has to be stealing anything deliberately? Look, downstairs we've charted all the data. Come and see it for yourselves. The pattern isn't the way a hoist ring operates. It *is* the way that bugs spread diseases. There's an expert on his way here who can tell you about it."

Grauss waved his hands in small circles like a Mississippi sidewheeler stranded on a mud bank. "But mit der aliens, ve haff ze *motive, ja?* Der time do zey vant to live easy, pecause der technology zey haff to take. But pugs? Vy der time do zese pugs vant?" He gestured toward Kopeksky. "Iss fir essen, he says? To eat? How eat zey der time?" He turned his hand upward and shrugged scornfully. "Vat nutritional value iss der time? How many calories iss vun hour?"

Kopeksky shook his head. "I'm not saying they eat time—"

"Vat ziss?" Grauss interrupted, throwing out a hand. "Virst he say der pugs, zey do eat der time. Now zey don't eat der time. Iss makink up der mind you should be, not vastink vat time iss left dat der aliens haff not taken."

"To *them* it's not time," Kopeksky persisted. "In their universe, they eat some kind of food, sure. But what I'm saying is that with all these dimensions and stuff, maybe it gets altered somehow and looks like time to us."

"They could convert one to another," Deena interjected in an effort to clarify. "Maybe in the same kind of way that energy and mass are interconvertible within our universe ... Or space and time between Einsteinian reference frames."

Grauss blinked. Wade stared at her in astonishment. Hasley nodded.

"I think there might be grounds here for a basic policy review for the entire investigation," Langlon said in a tone that sounded as if that wrapped the whole thing up, right there. Nobody took any notice.

"How zis food unt der time, zey transform?" Grauss challenged. But at the same time, he was twiddling uncomfortably with the marker pen and sounding less sure of his ground.

"I dunno," Kopeksky answered. "That's your department. But instead of saying they can't and putting the brakes on everything before you've even started, why not say maybe they do and try working backward? Then see where that gets you."

"Inductive, not deductive," Deena pointed out, being helpful in case anyone had missed it.

"It could form a complete transform group," Hasley murmured, more to himself.

"How did we ever get into this shit?" Wade groaned, looking perplexedly around the room from one to another.

The intercom on Langlon's desk buzzed. He stared at it with the paralyzed expression of a human cannonball watching the net go sailing by below. "Better answer it," Wade suggested.

Langlon reached out and pressed a button. "Yes, Betty?"

His secretary's voice replied from the outer office. "I'm sorry to interrupt again, Mr. Langlon, but there are two gentlemen here wanting to see Mr. Kopeksky and Mr. Wade. I told them you're in conference, but they are being most insistent. One of them is a priest, and the man with him—"

"They're the guys I'm expecting," Kopeksky said. Langlon shot Wade an inquiring look. Wade nodded resignedly in a way that said this couldn't get any worse.

"Show them in, please," Langlon said to the intercom and clicked it off.

The door opened and Moynihan came in, followed by Erringer. "You're taking your life in your hands crossing the street out there, and that's for sure," Moynihan said. "It's like Lansdowne Road in Dublin when the Brits beat Ireland at rugby."

Betty hovered guiltily in the doorway behind them, looking like an embarrassed beaver whose dam had fallen down. "I'm sorry, Mr. Langlon, but they were most insistent. . . ." Langlon nodded that it was okay and waved a hand. Betty left, closing the door.

Kopeksky introduced everybody. Erringer's news was that the Scicomp Building had been declared unsafe and evacuated, and city engineers were now examining the Queensboro Bridge adjacent to it, which had apparently contracted similar problems. He had heard the gist of Kopeksky's idea from Moynihan on the way across town and was intrigued. "Well, whatever else, it sure fits" was the only judgment he was prepared to pass at this stage, however.

Grauss wasn't prepared to let another scientist onto the territory without some show of credentials. "Vy zen zese patches do ve see all over der city? Vy zese pugs, zey eat time from here unt from here, but not eat it from zere unt from zere?" he queried, waving an arm first on one side, then the other. "Vy der Pell Telephone's time zey eat, unt der JFK time zey eat, but der time from der Park unt der basepall stadiums unt der churches zey don't eat? Vass iss difference? Time iss time, nein? Vere iss sense? Makes no sense."

Wade looked at Erringer curiously. Erringer just shrugged.

There was a short silence. Then Deena said, "I wonder what Eskimos would say if they knew we had all kinds of different words for construction material."

Wade shook his head as if to clear it. "What?"

"Well, you know, maybe this is like with Eskimos . . . To us it's just snow, but they've got I don't know how many different words for it, because to them it serves many different purposes." She looked around quickly, as if seeking moral support. The others returned expressions totally devoid of encouragement or comprehension. She went on, anyway. "Time could work the same way with these bugs that we're talking about. For us it's just"—she made clutching motions in the air as if groping for a word, then gave up—" 'time,' it's all the same. But for them there might be different kinds of time." She nodded to herself as if finally getting straight in her head what she wanted to say. "What I mean is, they could see it as different kinds of . . . whatever it is they eat—but it all looks like the same 'time' to us. Or I guess you could say that they see different kinds of time, where we don't. So the reason why they eat it from some places and not others is that different kinds of time somehow . . . 'taste' better."

" 'Taste better'?" Wade repeated the words, thought about them, shook his head, and looked at Langlon. Grauss stood hunched like some scrawny bird of prey, his fingers curled around the marker like talons.

"If it's a total transform group, who knows what might happen?" Hasley said at last, still distantly. "If matter in their universe can transform into something as apparently unrelated as time in ours, who's to say what variations there might be about time that make it as different as chalk from cheese to these bugs?"

"Or granite from wood," Moynihan said, taking the point and nodding. "Tastes different to them, eh? My word, there's thought enough for a few wet Sundays in all this."

"Something qualitatively different about different kinds of time that gives it a different . . . flavor," Hasley completed. He spread his hands to show that that was as far as he could take it.

Everyone seemed to be waiting on everyone else for an inspiration. Erringer paced slowly over to the window and looked out. The others watched but said nothing.

"Why not?" he announced finally, and turned to face them. "Deena said that time looks all the same to us, but does it really? I know that the instruments we physicists measure time with don't distinguish one kind from another. But isn't it true that we, as beings who are far more cognitive than any instrument, are well aware that time comes in all manner of brands and flavors?" He paused and looked around invitingly, as if to allow the others to add something. Then he indicated the priest with a nod. "Father Moynihan here just said it. We all know the difference between how time drags on a wet Sunday and flies when you're enjoying yourself at a party; or a morning spent waiting for an appointment with the dentist and one rushing to an airport. See what I mean? We all *know* that different kinds of time feel different. They even seem to run at different rates. Well, conceivably the differences in time in our universe that correspond to whatever these bugs base their preferences on in theirs have to do with just that: what's *happening in it!*"

Now it was Deena's turn to look confused. "You mean different things happening in what we see as time? That's what gives it a different flavor to them?"

"Right," Erringer said.

Moynihan pinched his nose dubiously. "What's happening in it?" he repeated. "Are you telling us that day-to-day affairs that would only have meaning to men and their maker could be of significance to microbes? Ah, now, that's too much for me to be swallowing. I don't think I could go along with that at all, at all."

Erringer shook his head. "No, I didn't mean that they're sensitive to events that are meaningful only at the subjective human level. That was just to illustrate the point. But quantities that are objectively measurable, such as rates of change of various physical variables, do give different intervals of time distinctly different characteristics, which might equate to properties that the bugs in the other universe can distinguish between."

"All right, I'm with you now," Moynihan said, giving the notion his blessing.

"Such as rate of change of electric field!" Hasley exclaimed. "Especially when in regular patterns, and with overall power density figuring in somehow as a secondary variable. Which is what we've already said characterizes the worst-affected sites."

"I think you've got it," Erringer said, moving back from the window.

Hasley nodded rapidly as a lot more pieces of the picture fell into place. "It would explain the whole pattern that we've been seeing," he said. "Not only why it happens most at places like computer sites or TV centers, but also why things improve when they shut down: the bugs lose their appetite and go feed someplace else."

"And why the effect is smaller at less active installations, such as smaller computer sites, nighttime telephone exchanges, and even individual electronic appliances," Erringer said.

Kopeksky held his hands up and looked in amazement at the two watches he was still wearing, one on each wrist. "You mean that's why this piece of digital junk falls behind the windup? There's bugs actually being attracted to the electronics . . . that are eating the time there?"

"Exactly," Erringer said.

"Jeez!" Kopeksky breathed, staring fixedly at his

chronometer as if he half expected to see them buzzing around it.

"And why there was nothing at all at St. Vitus," Moynihan said. "Everything of ours is clockwork, the way God intended."

Kopeksky frowned. "But wait a minute. If that's so, then how come my windup watch was behind yours when I was there earlier?"

"You'd just come from Scicomp," Erringer said. Kopeksky failed to look any the wiser. Erringer explained, "The time loss is worst at the innards of equipment that produces the conditions that the bugs find tastiest—in other words at the cores of the busiest parts of the machines, where there are more of them consuming it and presumably reproducing."

That made sense. Kopeksky nodded. "So that's why the red haze started in places like that," he guessed.

"Yes. Let's call that the 'core time.' So the depletion begins at the core, and hence in the early stages you get electronics running slow and all the effects that we observed, but outside the cabinets and in the immediate surroundings you don't see anything abnormal. But if I'm correct, this depletion at the core creates something like a 'time hole,' which causes time to fall into it, as it were, from the surrounding vicinity, and eventually the loss becomes perceptible in the room outside and the region around in general."

"And I'd spent some time in a place that was affected like that. So the watch I was carrying registered it. Okay." Kopeksky nodded to say that he was prepared to buy that much.

Erringer went on. "And if the parallel in our universe is anything to go by, the bug population increases, and the effect continues to spread outward from there."

And what after that? Kopeksky wondered. It *was* like a termite attack. Things appeared normal until a state of imminent collapse was reached, and then suddenly everything started falling in at once.

"*And that is why your cousin May,/ Fell through the parlor floor today,*" Moynihan murmured absently to himself. Evidently he had arrived at the same conclusion.

"From the measurements I saw at Scicomp, the local time outside the machine cabinets was slipping by about twenty percent," Erringer said. "That's just about the figure you'd need to shift the normal spectrum of visible wavelengths into the red. And again, that's just what was observed."

Kopeksky gave Wade a satisfied look. Whatever that meant, it sounded as if it confirmed his theory. "See," he said, making his voice sound as if it should have been obvious all along.

Wade and Langlon exchanged questioning looks. The others waited, having said all there really was to say. "What do you think?" Wade asked finally.

"I don't know. It's ... I guess it's just about the craziest thing I've ever heard."

Wade nodded. "Me too. In fact, it's just crazy enough that it might be true." He shrugged, as if excusing himself for stating the obvious. "But you get to expect that with Joe." Kopeksky grunted and raised his eyebrows at Deena.

Grauss was looking uncertainly from Erringer to Hasley to Kopeksky and then back again. For a moment he seemed to be tottering on the edge of reconsidering, but then he rallied and pounced on the point that was still unanswered. "Unt vy, zen, now der puildings zey fall down? Iss it der pugs now der city are consumink? Eizer zey eat der time or zey eat New York. Now iss both? Iss dat vat ve are now to believe, you are askink us?"

"That's the part I'm not too clear on either," Kopeksky admitted.

"Of course, I shall expect a full report on all this," Langlon said, having duly considered his options. His desk intercom buzzed. He answered it. "Yes?"

This time Betty didn't bother apologizing but answered in an unquestioning tone that sounded resigned to accepting that everyone in the building would eventually end up in Langlon's office. "Jack Orelli from the materials lab. He's got the results of some tests they've been doing down there that Mr. Kopeksky said couldn't wait."

"Send him in," Langlon said.

A broad-chested, swarthy man in white shirtsleeves came in, carrying a wad of handwritten notes and figures and a folder. He singled out Kopeksky and opened the folder to reveal X-ray pictures and micrographs. "I'll tell you one thing, Joe, right up front, and that's that nobody downstairs has seen anything like these before," he said.

Kopeksky nodded toward Erringer. "I'm just the mailman for this one, Jack. That's who you should tell it to—Dr. Erringer, from an outfit called Scicomp, which is where the stuff came from. And this is Father Moynihan, who's helping us out. I guess you know everyone else."

Orelli selected some of the pictures and addressed Erringer. "There aren't any signs of what you'd call normal material deterioration. In cases of metallic corrosion or decomposition of concrete, you expect to find evidence of chemical activity and decay products.

But here we don't have any. No signs of chemical changes. The materials are all of regular composition, but they're deformed. In every case the microstructure is altered in a way that I've never heard of before."

"No chemical reactions?" Erringer repeated. "So you're saying there's no actual material deficit? What accounts for the loss of mechanical strength, then?"

"That's exactly it." Orelli spread some of the plates out on Langlon's desk. "There's no loss of mass. But the density is reduced. It's as if all those materials—the steel tubes there, one of the bearings here, a sample of the concrete in this one—have been turned into microscopic Styrofoam somehow. They're full of holes."

"You mean like sponge, Jack?" Deena said, looking puzzled. So did everyone else.

"On a much smaller scale," Orelli replied. "I'm talking about way, way smaller than that—as I said, microscopic." He picked out another micrograph and pointed. "Look there. In that piece of metal the interstices occur between the crystal grains, which have all been displaced. So what was an internally cohesive material turns into popcorn. That's where all its strength went."

Wade told himself that he might as well stick a toe in the water with all this scientific stuff too. What the hell? Everyone else was trying it. "Then it sounds as if what we said earlier was wrong," he ventured. "These bugs *are* eating the buildings as well, after all. Like with the termites."

But Orelli shook his head. "No. The holes aren't there because of anything that's been eating the material away. It's more as if the holes were *added* to what was already there." He looked up, showed his palms, and shook his head as a disclaimer. "It's as if tiny volumes of space had been *created* somehow, all the way through the material. That causes the mass to expand and distort, which is why all your bearings and motors seized up."

"Let me get this straight," Kopeksky said. "You're saying that there's holes in there, but not because anything got eaten away. All the stuff that was there before is still there now. But the holes just started appearing . . . like outta nowhere?"

Orelli threw his hands out. "That's exactly it, Joe. What else can I tell ya? It's got us beat."

"And it's spreading out from the primary sites and affecting nearby structures like the Queensboro Bridge," Erringer said distantly. "Where do the holes come from? Where does the time go?" He seemed at a loss. He focused back inside the room and turned questioningly toward Moynihan, but the priest was looking equally baffled.

"What happens to the wood that termites eat, anyhow?" Kopeksky asked, more to fill the void than with any constructive thought in mind.

"They metabolize it into gas, mostly," Moynihan replied. "Mainly carbon dioxide."

"Hm."

And then Grauss, who had gone quiet while absorbing it all like a crossbow slowly bending under tension, suddenly had his moment of conversion. *"Ja! Mein gott, ja!"* he exclaimed, springing upright and startling everyone else in the room. "At vonce der complete picture do I see. In der other dimensional universe, vat ve haff a time unt space, zey are convertible. Unt der pugs, zey metabolize der vun into der other. As der time it iss input, but turned into space it outputs. Unt der space is diffused like mit der termite gases."

He looked proudly at Erringer. "*Ja? Nein?* Vat off dat, Dr. Erringer, you zink?"

"What's he saying?" Wade asked, mystified.

Erringer could only shake his head incredulously. "That the bugs eat time and excrete space," he replied. "The way that things project into our universe, their metabolic process converts one into the other. It's the craziest thing I've heard all day. And this has been some day."

Grauss threw his arms up in exasperation. "Vy you say iss crazy?" he objected. "Everybody I listen to today iss crazy. Der zings vat you say too, dey are crazy, unt vat he says, unt vat she says, unt vat he says. So vy not I can be crazy? But all together ve make sense. See . . ." He turned back to the whiteboard and cleaned it with a series of rapid sweeps of the eraser pad.

"Didn't I say something like this?" Deena said to the room, but everyone was watching Grauss.

Grauss put down the eraser and turned to gaze at the blank board. "Virst ve assume der governing equation to be off similar form to der Einstein relationship for der space unt der time, like so," he said, scrawling the familiar $E=mc^2$ at the top. "So, ve take space, vich iss volume, or length cubed, equated to der light velocity squared." He added a further line of symbols, looked at them, and shook his head. "But in dimensions ve see zat der two sides do not balance. Vor completeness ve must insert here der factor havink dimensions of length multiplied by time." He carried on, swiftly adding more lines with calculus operators. "Unt here, from der velocity expression, ve see zat der factor iss identical mit der time-integral of distance. Unt now ve ask, vat quantity it iss ve know dat hass such dimensions?" He looked around expectantly like a professor in a lecture room, as if answers should already be pouring back from all directions.

"He needs a factor to balance the equation," Erringer informed the others. "And it has to have the dimensions of length times time. From basic mechanics you can express it as the time-integral of distance. Or to put it in English, what is it that increases with time when nothing's happening?"

"Boredom," Deena answered automatically, without really thinking.

Langlon's intercom buzzed again. "The chief commissioner is on the line," Betty announced. "He's got the mayor on the line, who's got the state governor on his line, who's got the president on hold. The Queensboro Bridge has been closed and could collapse at any moment. One of the World Trade towers is starting to lean. Seven more buildings have been evacuated in the last half hour, and the streets around twelve city blocks have been closed. They want to know what you're going to do about it." Langlon stared at the unit with an expression that would have won a fish on a slab an animation prize. "What do I tell them?" Betty's voice asked. Her tone was flat and deadpan, as if she were preparing for someone else to reply that Langlon had jumped out of the window. A morguelike stillness enveloped the room.

"Well, what do you do to get rid of bugs?" Wade asked at last, more because somebody had to say something. He lifted a hand halfheartedly. "What can you do? . . . You can spray them, poison them. What else? . . ."

"Take out the nests," Kopeksky tried. "Find something else that eats them. . . ." He shook his head. "Nah." Nothing like that was going to get them anywhere, and they all knew it.

And then Hasley said, "Look I don't know if this makes any sense, but if these bugs . . . or whatever they are . . . like to eat time that's got electrical activity going on in it, then maybe time without anything electrical happening in it is"—he shrugged—"nonnutritional."

Erringer looked up sharply and stared at him. "What are you saying? That we might be able to starve them?"

Hasley nodded. "Something like that." He shrugged again and looked around. If everyone else was into crazy things today, then that was his nickel's worth.

Erringer looked at Langlon, who was still sitting with a finger on a button of the silently waiting intercom. "It's a thought," Erringer said. "At least it gives us something to say to them. And who knows? It might even work."

But it didn't.
 Kopeksky stood with Erringer and Deena in the main control room of Con Edison's Energy Control Center on the West Side of Manhattan. This was the nerve center that directed the switching and routing of power from thirteen generating plants in the New York City area and coordinated their operation with the six other utilities that formed the statewide New York Power Pool. The same center also supervised the distribution of natural gas across the area, as well as controlling the supply of piped process steam to over two thousand customers.

The panel above them in the series of huge mimic displays overlooking the floor of control desks and monitor consoles showed the power supply grid covering Union and Essex counties, New Jersey. In the center of the sector lay Newark International Airport and its immediate environs, which had been selected for the experiment. It had been cut off from all power, isolated. The hope had been that if all electrical activity in the vicinity ceased, the mysterious alien "chronovores," as the scientists had now dubbed them, would famish and die out, or else migrate elsewhere in whatever peculiar realm they inhabited. But the reports from the scientists ringing the area with crystal-controlled timers and frequency standards locked to transmissions from outside showed that the bugs were simply migrating outward from Newark in search of new forage. The measures were not only failing to eradicate the plague, but actually spreading it faster.

"Well, it might have worked," Erringer said. He was feeling particularly glum just then. On the other side of town, the Scicomp Building had collapsed that morning. Wall Street was missing a few teeth, and only the Triborough and George Washington bridges were still operating, both of them down to single lanes.

Hasley turned from a table with a large map spread out on top, where a group of scientists and city engineers were plotting the information coming in from the measuring stations set up across the river. Coordinating with the external world was a feat in itself, since the core dilation of the systems inside the Con Edison Center was averaging around sixty percent. It meant that everything in the outside world was running over half again as fast, and they were constantly having to reset their clocks to catch up.

"They're latching on to whatever they encounter," Hasley announced. "Some trucks have been stopped carrying them down the turnpike with their CBs. In other places it's personal computers and TVs, even portable radios. If this goes it'll turn into a national epidemic. We'll be sending carriers all over the country."

The director in charge of operations took stock of the situation from his seat in the center of a master desk on a raised dais overlooking the room. "Abort the whole thing," he instructed. "We're just making a big fan and throwing shovelfuls at it. This way it'll be in California by tomorrow."

"What do we do about the test sector?" one of the aides beside him asked, meaning the airport and its surroundings.

"Turn everything back on. It'll give the bugs something to chew on. At least that way we'll know where they are until somebody figures out what to try next."

Deena looked unhopefully at Kopeksky. "Any thoughts what to try next?" she asked.

"Go find a hot dog stand or something," Kopeksky growled. "All this talk about starving bugs has made me hungry."

"A drop o' the dew of Tullamore," Father Moynihan said. Kopeksky watched from one of the armchairs in the priest's study as Moynihan leaned over the side table between them and poured two glasses of Irish whiskey. He motioned at a jug beside the glasses. "You can add water to suit your taste. I just take a splash meself."

Kopeksky decided to try it straight. It was warm and mellow, a lot smoother than he had expected. Didn't hit the back of the throat with diesel fumes, like scotch. He suspected that Moynihan might have pulled off another conversion.

"I, ah, take it that it's all right?" Moynihan said,

pausing as he lifted his own glass and looked up. "Ye being on duty and that, I mean."

Kopeksky heaved his shoulders and sighed. "What the hell? The way things are going, there won't be much more duty in this city to be worrying about for very much longer." He took another sip. "How about you? On duty it's okay?"

Moynihan smiled. "Ah, well, now, in our line of work we're on duty, as it were, all the time. Therefore we have to be, what one might call, a little more pragmatic about these matters."

"And to fit in back home, right?" Kopeksky offered, to give Moynihan an even broader excuse.

"Ah, now don't ye be so quick at slagging us," Moynihan said. "We're a very devout and holy breed, I'll have you know. Why, doesn't every Irishman try to model his life on that of Christ?"

"How'd you figure that?"

"Ye've only got to look at them. They're still living at home at the age of thirty. All with twelve good drinking buddies, faithful and true. And there isn't a one among them where both he and his mother doesn't think that he's God. . . . Anyhow, it isn't the best of news that ye've brought, I gather. The experiment they tried at Newark didn't work?"

"It made things even worse." Kopeksky went on to summarize what had happened. He ended, tossing out a hand wearily, "So they had to call it off. It was all ready to take off across the state."

Moynihan, who had been listening intently, nodded over his still quarter-full glass. "That's just what it was by the sound of it. The microbes were finding carriers. We should have guessed, if we'd thought about it, from the way those two watches that you carry get out of step. It's only a small difference, I know, but it means that the electronic one manages to draw a few of them to itself. That would be enough to grow into a large population again, as soon as they found a larger source of food."

"You mean they could follow a person's watch?" Kopeksky looked horrified. "Maybe hitch a ride on a plane someplace, like rats on a ship? And then start breeding again when they got to a big IBM center or somewhere? It works like that?"

"That's the way it's beginning to sound to me, all right. A classic case of carrier transmission."

Kopeksky shook his head protestingly. "Well ... hell. What do you do about it?"

"Quarantine is the first step, of course. Strict quarantine. Thank God the airports closed when they did, or else it might have been everywhere by now. But you have to stop those people who are moving out of the city and into the state and elsewhere from taking anything electronic with them. Call in all the radios, TVs, calculators, everything. And keep a strict watch for outbreaks in other places they might have taken it to already, and contain them too."

"That doesn't sound too easy," Kopeksky said uneasily.

"I never said it would be."

"Okay, suppose we manage it. Then what?"

Moynihan shrugged. "You apply any measures you know of to kill it ..."

"We don't."

"... in which case you can only wait for it to die out."

"What if it doesn't?"

"It has to eventually. Every organism depends on

some source of nourishment. If you cut that source off, it stands to reason that the infection must terminate."

"I thought you said the Irish didn't always care too much about what stands to reason."

"They don't. But fortunately with reality it's a different matter."

Kopeksky watched the flames in the fireplace and considered the proposition. It didn't sound very encouraging. "We could end up sending the whole world back to the Stone Age before we're through," he murmured.

"Then maybe we'll make a better job of getting out of it the second time round," Moynihan said.

Kopeksky stared at the fire. "You might even end up with fields around again. . . . So there's not a lot else. Nothing more sort of . . . positive?" He looked back across the room, sensing that Moynihan wasn't listening. The priest was lost in thought, staring through the hearth rug. "Hello?" Kopeksky tried cautiously.

"Rats," Moynihan said, still with a faraway expression.

"What?"

Moynihan returned part of the way. "You compared them to rats a minute ago. I'd never thought of that. I've always had this vision of them in me mind as insects."

"So?"

Moynihan came back fully and turned in his chair. "Maybe there is something better that we can do," he said. "If these creatures that we're talking about find time with electrical activity going on in it to be so tasty, then perhaps we can arrange a really irresistible morsel or two that will enable us to send them away somewhere else." His eyes glittered in the firelight. "I'm sure you've heard the story about a fella known as the Pied Piper from a long time ago, in a little place they called Hamelin. . . ."

It was possibly the most outlandish cavalcade ever to have trundled its way along a U.S. public highway. In the middle, an army field tractor hauled one of the enormous flatbed trailers designed for transporting the M1 Abrahams Main Battle Tank. On it, surrounded by the now familiar reddish haze, were mounted a double line of steel cabinets containing a collection of some of the most powerful computer hardware available, obtained from sites all over the New York City metropolitan area. A mobile generating system coupled behind supplied power, while trucks ahead, behind, and on the flanks carried teams of scientists with equipment to measure fluctuations of time dilation in the immediate vicinity.

Kopeksky was back in Con Edison's control center, watching as the situation around Newark was reconstructed on one of the mural displays above the lines of control desks. Once again the power to the area centered upon the airport had been switched off, and the chronovores had moved outward to its periphery to form localized clusters around small computer setups, neon signs, telephone switchboards, hi-fi stores—anything that offered something to nibble on until their next opportunity for a hearty meal. "Sweeper One," as the mobile installation on the flatbed trailer had been designated, was just passing an automated bottling plant south of the airport, where one of the centers of localized time dilation had been detected.

"Flank Right is reporting a dip. I think we've got it. Looks like they might be moving," a controller at one of the monitors sang out. A tense expectancy rose around the room. On the dais the operations director and his staff sat motionless, waiting.

"Station Seventeen reporting now," another voice called. That was the measuring post inside the bottling plant. "Their lag is reducing already, slipping back to EST . . . oh, fast, fast!" The swarm had caught the scent of the passing meal wagon and were pouring out after it.

"Trail has a dip. They're following."

A voice high with surprise: "Seventeen's heading for zero. This is incredible! It can work that fast?"

"Andy, get a second check on that reading from Seventeen and report." The director's voice this time.

A pause. Then, "Yep, they're clean there. No question about it."

Kopeksky turned toward where Moynihan was standing next to him. "Do you hear what I hear?" he muttered disbelievingly. "I'm starting to think that this crazy idea of yours might really work."

"Ah, what are ye talking about? 'Twas a grand idea, to be sure, to be sure."

For the rest of the day Sweeper One lumbered around the periphery of the airport area, adding more chronovore swarms to its catch. And all along its route the digital watches, clock radios, and other devices that had been showing minor time lags all ceased misbehaving, which seemed to indicate that as everyone had hoped but none had dared predict, the strays along the way were being swept up too.

By nightfall all of the measuring posts around the quarantined zone were reporting null results, and Sweeper One had crossed the turnpike and traversed the industrial parks and railroad sidings of Jersey City to the west bank of the Hudson. From there, moving with agonizing slowness in its own cocoon of fifty percent retarded time, the convoy led its strange following through the Holland Tunnel and back into Manhattan. By the next morning all readings were still showing the Jersey side to be clean.

In the Con Edison Energy Control Center, the operations director sat back at his desk up on the dais and looked satisfied. "It looks as if we're good on the test run," he told his lieutenants sitting on either side. "Okay, let's try for the big one while we've still got some of this city left. Alert all zone controllers and copy the governor's office. We're going straight to EXTERMINATOR right now. Get the activation plan up on the screens."

00:13

New York City lay wrapped in an unheard-of stillness. Its towers stood empty and silent like the stones of a gigantic, forgotten graveyard. Every window of the stores and office blocks was unlit; not a neon sign flickered; nor did a traffic light wink, an elevator move, or a motor hum, anywhere. The entire electrical supply to the city had been shut off and the use of battery-powered devices of any kind banned. The hospitals had been evacuated, the businesses closed, and most of the residents had left for surroundings that offered some vestige of the comforts and conveniences that they were accustomed to. Detachments of police and Guard patrolled the streets to enforce the emergency regulations and protect property from looting. Scientists had set up a network of stations to record the vicissitudes of local times, and engineers were maintaining a constant watch for further instances of failing structures. But apart from them, only a few, through curiosity, obstinacy, or simply the elevated feeling that some people experience from being different, remained to wander through the parks or along the deserted avenues, reveling in the solitude, feasting on the silence, or stopping occasionally to take in the spectacle of sagging floors exposed by the collapsed side of a skyscraper or a street filled with the rubble of what had yesterday been a whole building.

Wearing a nylon overjacket on top of his coat, Joe Kopcksky sat in a NYPD helicopter circling above the East River, just off the southern tip of Roosevelt Island. Moynihan was next to him, with Erringer and Deena in the two seats across the narrow center aisle. Wade and Grauss, along with several other scientific people and a couple of officials from Washington, filled the rear section of the cabin.

Below them, a short distance to the north, what looked like a deep red cloud lay on the Manhattan shoreline, just opposite the rear of what was left of the Scicomp Building, below the ruined west end of the Queensboro Bridge. The cloud enveloped a pair of huge barges lashed together and moored alongside FDR Drive. A flotilla of tugboats stood a short distance out on the fringe of the cloud, trailing thick towing lines back to the barges.

One of the barges was loaded with diesel engines, electrical generating equipment, and a pumping system to circulate cooling water. From it, a tangle of cables and hoses connected across to the other barge, which was fitted with a canvas canopy supported by posts. Beneath the canopy was a super version of the lure that had been tested as Sweeper One: an array of several hundred electronics cabinets jammed side by side in rows and stacked several tiers deep. The assortment included the supercomputers from Scicomp's basement, which had survived the collapse of the building; giant machines from the banks and Wall Street; heavy peripheral drivers from service bureaus and commercial sites; and processor-bound number crunchers from engineering centers, research institutes, and colleges. There were no disk drives or anything else mechanical to break down—just cubicles containing pure electronics, which would take days to deteriorate to the point of becoming nonfunctional. They didn't have to do anything that would normally be considered productive; only to run programs that would drive every piece of circuitry to its utmost.

Hence, at just this one spot in the entire New York City area, there existed a concentration of millions of the fastest electronic circuit chips that had ever been produced, switching tightly regimented patterns of data at a local power intensity that one of the engineers had described to Kopeksky as being like "half of IBM and Con Edison put on the Staten Island ferry."

The decks of the barges and the quay alongside them were scenes of hectic activity. At least, the observers in the swarm of helicopters overhead and on the boats dotted about the river were assured that what was going on down there was hectic activity. But through binoculars, the figures moving among the bundles of cables snaking all over the decks, waving direction from the tugs, or going up and down the gangplanks to the shore all seemed to drift about their tasks with a strange, dreamlike lethargy—an impression that at first sight seemed all the more objectionable on account of their being volunteers on a thousand dollars an hour. In fact, the time dilation in the vicinity of the barges was now running in excess of twenty-five percent, while the circuits at the core of the operating electronics were losing no less than forty-five minutes out of every hour.

In terms of sheer space concentration of electrical activity, it was the equivalent of an island of rain forest in the center of the Sahara, or a single supernova pouring out light into the intergalactic void. As a source of chronovore food, New York had been turned into a desert; and to entice its locust swarms away from whatever scraps and remnants they might have found across the metropolitan wilderness, a feast had been prepared in the midst of the famine.

And it seemed to have worked. For days now, the scientists across the city had been measuring time returning to normal everywhere and a halt in the appearance of new cases of structural decay. As had happened with the trial scheme at Newark, some localized pockets had remained along the fringe of the area, and a fleet of lumbering Sweeper units had been going out, back and forth, all day long, bringing them back into the common pound. By now, no time losses were being reported from anywhere else, and the dilation around the barges had escalated to the highest that had been encountered. The Pied Piper had rounded up his catch. Now it was time to take them away.

A red dot appeared on the shoreline across the river from the barges, on the Queens side. It grew to become more distinct and then rose slowly to hang a couple of hundred feet above the command post that had been set up to coordinate the river part of the operation. The balloon was a signal that the final phase had received its go-ahead.

"There it is, folks," the pilot's voice shouted over the engine.

"*Ja*, see now. Ve haff der palloon," Grauss's voice said excitedly from behind.

Deena craned forward in her seat until she could pick it out herself over the rooftops. "That's it? So everything's clear now down there?"

"Let's hope so, anyhow," Erringer muttered next to her.

"Want me to go down and check it out?" the pilot asked.

"'Do that," Wade's voice said.

The helicopter banked into a turn and dipped toward the east shore. As it came closer, the observer up front with the pilot used binoculars to read the signal being run up on flag masts below. The helicopter was under strict radio silence, no use of radar allowed, no computers, no navigational electronics. Strictly seat-of-the-pants stuff, the way real flying used to be. And ditto, especially, for ground control and the other operations going on below, where communications were restricted to dispatch riders, semaphore, Morse lamps, and a minimum of rudimentary field telephones.

"*All clocks reporting in synch,*" the observer decoded. "*Final traces infestation appear eliminated. Proceeding Phase Green.*"

"Did ye hear that? The saints be praised!" Moynihan exclaimed. A burst of cheering and hand-clapping erupted from the rest of the cabin. Erringer turned and gave Deena a hug. Wade pounded the armrest of his seat solidly in satisfaction.

"Vy iss saints all off sudden?" Grauss asked, looking at Erringer. "Vat dey do to stop der pugs? Ve haff something to do mit also, a little, *ja*?"

"Ah, you know how it is with these PR guys," Kopeksky told him, indicating Moynihan with a jerk of his thumb.

The chopper climbed again and moved back toward the red cloud hanging over the barges on the Manhattan side. Already, the gangplanks to the shore were being lifted back. In the eerie shroud of red fading to smoky purple at the center, the figures on the decks moved in slow motion, hauling in lines, securing cables, and making last-minute checks and adjustments. Then the water at the sterns of the waiting tugs churned into orange foam—they were inside the fringe of the optically affected zone—and one by one the tugs began straining forward to take up the slack in the lines. Slowly, slowly from the viewpoint of those watching from overhead, the vessels formed into two fans of tugboats ahead of and pulling the pair of heavily laden barges. Still surrounded by the red cloud, which slowly detached itself from the shoreline, the strange armada moved out to the center of the East River and set course downstream. It passed under the Brooklyn Bridge and moved out into Upper New York Bay.

There it lay moored a mile out from the shore, bathed in its red aura, for a full week. During this period several chronovore swarms that had been missed were found on shore, lured away, and brought out to the barges by a floating version of the Sweepers. Finally, every test that could be devised failed to find any remaining trace of the affliction anywhere in Manhattan or its surrounding boroughs.

It was time for the final act. A freighter that had been specially prepared in South Brooklyn docks was brought out to the barges—a 20,000-ton container ship whose holds had been reinforced and made watertight and then fitted out with more banks of high-power computing hardware. The hardware aboard the barges, which by now was just about at the end of its span and had begun giving out, was shut down, and, exactly as planned, the accumulated swarm moved to the new concentration running flat-out in the freighter. The freighter was then towed to a point a thousand miles out above the North Atlantic deep and sunk. Five miles down, in the lightless, lifeless desert of the abyssal plain, everything switched off.

Utter stillness reigned. Utter silence. Nothing moving, nothing changing. Time eternal. Time with nothing happening in it. Bland time. Insipid time. Tasteless time. Nutritionless time.

And there, the chronovores starved.

All but a few, that is. In a separate compartment of the vessel, a personal computer was left running at a low activity level to keep a small, controlled population alive. Instruments would automatically adjust the running program to keep the numbers in check and report the situation periodically via a surface buoy satellite-linked to shore.

For as Erringer had pointed out, if such creatures existed, they posed a constant threat to any civilization that hoped to advance itself further. Hence there could well be a need to develop permanent means of monitoring and pest control to add to mankind's armory of weaponry to maintain his well-being. Hence, a few samples for future research would be worth preserving.

00:14

The traffic was flowing again—and snarling up, and hooting and honking—in New York City. It sounded good. There was still a lot of rubble to be shoveled up and some rebuilding to do, but on the whole, when it came to demonstrating its capacity for getting back to business as usual, humanity had excelled itself.

Kopeksky was just in the process of putting the last pages in his file to wrap up the case, when a call came from the Day Room to say that Moynihan was downstairs, asking to see him. "Yeah, sure. Send him up," Kopeksky said. "For him it's anytime, okay?"

"Who's that?" Deena asked from across the office as he put down the phone. The latest assignment from Wade was to look into the problem of a new kind of computer virus loose in the networks that was causing dire fundamentalist religious warnings to pop up without warning on screens everywhere. She and her purse were sandbagged behind piles of books on programming and communications, and a layer of manufacturer's catalogs and phone company literature had been added to the stratifications on her desk. She also, Kopeksky had noticed but not gone out of his way to mention, had turned up in a new, nicely balanced two-piece of beige and white trim, shoes that matched, and had coaxed her hair into an attractive ponytail.

"Moynihan," Kopeksky answered. "Maybe we're due for another delivery of tea."

"We're still only halfway through the first batch. Do you think I should heat up some water?"

"I wouldn't bother. It's almost lunchtime." Kopeksky looked over and nodded to indicate the semicircle of precariously balanced confusion at arm's length around Deena's chair. "How's it going with that stuff?"

"It's fascinating. By some definitions you could argue that these things are really alive. It makes me wonder if you could base a prosecution on sending live animals through the mail."

"Don't tell Grauss about it. He'd have everybody looking for a whole zoo." The last they'd heard, Grauss was busy following up a speculation of his that there might also exist bugs that operated on the inverse metabolism of feeding on empty space and turning it into time. If so, it might prove possible to harness them as the basis of a means for life extension and staving off old age.

"Shall I go and get him?" Deena offered.

"I think he knows his way by now. Anyway, isn't it supposed to be kind of a sign of hospitality with the Irish to tell people to walk right in?"

As if on cue, there was a light tap on the door, and Moynihan entered. He was once again in a black raincoat and carrying an umbrella. "Just on me rounds and passing this way," he greeted. "And a grand morning it is that I've brought ye. Ah, 'tis great to see the city itself again, the way God intended. You're both very busy, I see, so I won't be keeping you. I was wondering if you were done with the books that I left here. . . . They wouldn't have been a lot of use to you, I suspect, with the way things turned out."

"I think Deena just about went through every one," Kopeksky replied.

"They were interesting," Deena said. She got up, knocking over some of the books stacked by her chair, and began sorting Moynihan's out from among more folders and papers piled on a table in a corner. "I think I could use the extra space though. Here, these are all yours, I think. Will they be okay in this?"

Moynihan took the plastic bag that she produced from somewhere in her purse and helped her put the books into it. "That will do just fine. . . . What is it they've got ye's into now, if you don't mind my asking?"

"More bugs," Deena told him.

"Ah, no, you're pulling me leg."

"But strictly in this universe this time. Some people are being a nuisance with computer viruses."

"Is that a fact?"

"There's no rush. We were just about to break for lunch," Kopeksky said. "Care to join us? Where would be a good place to go?"

"Well, now, there does happen to be a place not far from here that has the best lamb this side of the water, and the Guinness could be from St. James's Gate in Dublin itself."

Kopeksky nodded. "Sounds good to me." He cocked an inquiring eye at Deena. "Wanna give it a try?"

Deena flushed and began sorting, totally unnecessarily, through papers that were lying on her desk. "Oh, that would be nice. But as it happens I'm already having lunch with Graham, if he stops by. . . . I mean, I know he is stopping by, but just in case nothing happens that means he can't . . . if you know what I mean."

"Ah, yes," Moynihan said, taking the bag of books and nodding.

"We'll come down with you as far as the door, anyhow," Kopeksky said.

They took the elevator down and came out into the main lobby of the building just as Erringer appeared from the street. He was wearing a crisp white shirt with diagonal stripe college tie and navy blazer, creased gabardines, and carrying a white raincoat folded over one arm. "Uh-huh," Kopeksky murmured to himself.

Erringer grinned a shade self-consciously to acknowledge the presence of Kopeksky and Moynihan. "It's good to see the city back together again," he said.

"With all of it keeping in time too," Kopeksky agreed.

"I'm borrowing this partner of yours for an hour or so," Erringer said, indicating Deena as they went out onto the street.

"That could be a problem," Kopeksky replied. "I think the department has a regulation that says you have to put in a requisition for something like that."

"What? Even for one of your consultants? I just helped you solve one of your most important cases."

"In that case, maybe you're exempt."

"Just as well. I was never much good at filling out forms, anyway."

"Get out of here," Kopeksky told them.

Erringer offered his arm. Deena slipped hers through, and they disappeared around the corner of the block.

"I guess that just leaves you and me," Kopeksky said to Moynihan. "Now what were you saying about that place with the Guinness?"

"I thought you were on duty," Moynihan answered.

"Well, there are days when I qualify for an exemption too. I just decided this is one of them. Hey, you've got the umbrella. Let me carry that bag."

The policeman and the priest walked away together and were lost among the avenue's midday crowd.

ABOUT THE AUTHOR

JAMES P. HOGAN was born in London in 1941. He worked as an engineer specializing in electronics and for several major computer firms before turning to writing full-time in 1979. Winner of the Prometheus Award, he has earned wide popularity and high praise for his novels with their blend of gripping storytelling, intriguing scientific concepts, and convincing speculation. Mr. Hogan currently makes his home in the Republic of Ireland.

JAMES P. HOGAN

"Zindell is fashioning an astonishing epic of our distant and eerie galactic future."—Robert Silverberg

The Broken God

by
David Zindell

On the winter world of Icefall, young Danlo has grown up among a tribe of humans genetically altered to lead a primitive existence. When his tribe is ravaged by plague, he is forced to give up this simple, spiritual life to journey across the frozen wastes to the fabled city of Neverness, the teeming center of a vast galactic civilization. Here, a great destiny beckons Danlo—to pilot a ship to the heart of the galaxy and battle a deadly bloom of light that is consuming worlds and suns as it races toward his planet. But first he must confront the legend of his true father, a bold adventurer who is worshipped as a god—and the terrible allure of becoming a god himself.

❏ THE BROKEN GOD (56450-1 * $5.99/$6.99 in Canada)